495

184

Oprah Winfrey

Marianne Ruuth

MELROSE SQUARE PUBLISHING COMPANY
LOS ANGELES, CALIFORNIA

Consulting Editors for Melrose Square
Raymond Friday Locke
James Neyland

Originally published by Melrose Square, Los Angeles.
©1996 by Holloway House.

Cover Painting: Jesse Santos
Cover Design: Matt von Kroeker

Oprah Winfrey

MELROSE SQUARE BLACK AMERICAN SERIES

CONTENTS

Chapter One

Heeeeeeere's Oprah!

Waves of "oooohs," "aaaahs," breathless exclamations, hollered requests, and yells of admiration were surging from the fans, armed with cameras, snacks, and patience, watching from behind ropes as stars galore walked up a red carpet.

It was the NAACP 27th Image Awards—with the motto "From This Moment On"—on April 6, 1996, the purpose being to honor those who have contributed to the positive portrayal of African Americans in motion pictures, television, literature, and recording. Arriving early were the hosts, Denzel

---

Oprah Winfrey is about as famous as anyone can get, not only known throughout the world but honored with numerous awards. The honors are well deserved, for she has earned her fame through years of hard work and achievement.

Washington and Whitney Houston, followed by favorites such as LeVar Burton, Ice-T, LL Cool J, Quincy Jones, Martin Lawrence, Della Reese, Malik Yoba, Tisha Campbell, Robert Townsend, Eartha Kitt, Lela Rochon, Mykelti Williamson, Tatyana M. Ali, Alfre Woodard, Laurence Fishburne, Luther Vandross, Brandy, Boyz II Men, Loretta Divine, Angela Bassett, Cicely Tyson, Richard Pryor (who said later, when receiving the Hall of Fame Award, "I appreciate it but it's long overdue"), Arsenio Hall, Jesse Jackson, and many more.

At one moment, a change came over the crowd: Oprah had arrived, sleek in black, her phosphorescent smile competing with the setting California sun.

The fans' welcome to her was the kind you give an old friend, complete with big grins, a touch of familiarity and approval: "How'ya doing, girlfriend?" "Looking good, real good!" "Go, girl, go!"

They felt they really knew her—after all, hadn't she come into their living rooms, telling childhood secrets and speaking directly to them? "True, people tend to treat me like I'm their close friend," she has noted. "I think it's because I'm aware of the common bond we all share. My theory is that everybody is the same, wants the

At the NAACP's 27th Image Awards, Oprah presented the top award to Quincy Jones, her friend and mentor, a man of many talents and accomplishments, from performer to composer to producer and businessman.

Boyz II Men, the smash hit vocal group from Philadelphia, continued on the road to success by picking up a 1996 Image Award from the NAAC P in the category of Outstanding Duo or Group,

for their album II. *The individual members of the group are (above, left to right) Wanya Morris, Nathan Morris, Shawn Stockman, and Michael McCary.*

same—to be loved."

She is beyond being famous.

What is fame anyway? Whatever it is, she's got it.

Oprah Winfrey is so famous that she doesn't ever need to use her last name, not only in the United States but in a hundred countries throughout the world.

She is so famous that, when she visited a public restroom for the purposes that are the same for famous and non-famous folks, she was greeted with applause by the women at the sinks after she exited the stall!

She is so famous that the sober *Yale Law Journal* (in their January 1996 issue) used the term "Oprahfication"—meaning "to be guided by feelings."

She is so famous that she gets between two thousand and four thousand letters a week and people try to hug her in airplanes and on the street.

She is so famous that people feel they have the right to have strong opinions not just about her achievements and activities but about her weight, clothes, taste in companions, decision to marry or not, to have children or not, or any other private issue. The tabloids will criticize what she had for breakfast during a vacation trip—*What?*

The versatile, multi-talented Ice-T was presented a 1996 NAACP Image Award for Outstanding Supporting Actor in a Drama Series, for his performance in New York Undercover.

Upside-down pineapple pancakes dripping with syrup! Shame on her!—or declare they like her better chubby!

She is a bit suspicious when it comes to fame in today's world. "We honor people not because of their achievements but just because they are famous," she said recently.

Not so in her own case—achievement might be her middle name. The fact that she has earned her place in the sun by sweat and struggle, unflinching determination, and at the same time guarding her soul, is part of her charisma. So is her willingness to take risks, her empathetic personality and her ability to create an atmosphere of emotion and intimacy with people she does not know personally.

Fierce intelligence, down-to-earth common sense, and a humorous sparkle in her eye are other ingredients of her appeal and telegenic charm, right there for all to see just about every day on television, where she remains the queen of talk, equally at home with First Lady Hillary Clinton or a homeless person. It shows at other times, such as when chatting with stars before the Academy Awards in 1996, receiving a Chicago Bulls jersey from Dennis Rodman after the play-off game opposite the New

Jesse Jackson was in eloquent form at the 1996 NAACP Image Awards, where Both Sides with Jesse Jackson, *a talk show presented as part of CNN's* The Million Man March, *was nominated. The winner in the category was* The Oprah Winfrey Show.

York Knicks on May 7, 1996, or presenting others with awards.

She was chosen to make the presentation to her dear friend and valued mentor, Quincy Jones, the recipient of the NAACP's top Image Award, Entertainer of the Year, at the above-mentioned star-studded event.

The same night Oprah took home an Image award for her "Black for a Day" show, and in May she added to her long list of honors when she accepted a George Foster Peabody Award (recognizing broadcast and cable excellence) for personal achievement, and then another Emmy (Where does she put them all?) for her show.

This is the woman who grew up wanting to be Diana Ross but, realizing she would never have Miss Ross's thighs, she decided to be herself.

It worked beyond all expectations, although her road was bumpy at times. Against heavy odds, she dared, she broke the mold, she reached high, and she keeps going. "I love to be underestimated," she says impishly.

She can usually be found in the multi-faceted city of Chicago, once the home of notorious gangster Al Capone (in the 1920s), the site of the world's first nuclear chain reaction (1942), an inspiration to poet Carl

Image Award nominee Cicely Tyson (for her outstanding acting performance in Sweet Justice *on NBC) received a big hug from her friend Oprah, with whom she worked in* Brewster Place.

Sandburg (*Chicago Poems*), the birthplace of playwright Lorraine Hansberry, filmmaker Melvin Van Peebles, and musicman/producer Quincy Jones; also the city with the second-largest population of African Americans (1.4 million according to the census takers in 1990—only New York with 2.1 million tops that figure).

Inside a building, a block long, in beautiful downtown Chicago, housing a 100,000-square-foot state-of-the-art production studio with three sound stages, screening room, several offices, and a gym, *The Oprah Winfrey Show* is created—in her own image, as it were.

The minute she enters with a cheery "Hello, audience," a magnetic field of energy is unleashed. As red lights are blinking, she chats away with those who have come to see, hear, and participate. She might shoo off the producer, who is eager to begin taping. "Let me talk to these folks. They got up at four in the morning to be here, after all," she says.

On a regular basis, she demonstrates her gift of getting people to talk—about anything. A good family feeling radiates from her persona, fills the studio, and is passed on to the viewers as she interacts with her guests, being somber, empathetic, funny,

Oprah's vibrant personality attracts attention wherever she goes. Here she performs for photographers and news cameramen at the opening of Planet Hollywood

teasing, sincere, concerned, outraged, breaking down in tears, or handing out self-revelations and hugs.

Sometimes the feeling of comfort grows so strong and mutual that she invites her audience to lunch somewhere—or orders pizza to be delivered.

As talk shows keep proliferating rapidly, frequently resorting to shock TV, Oprah sees clearly the difference between being controversial and being sleazy. Controversy might begin a discussion and open eyes. Sleazy? Not her style. Neither is the idea of hurting people.

She told *Entertainment Weekly* in 1994 that a turning point came one day in 1989 when she had a wife, a husband, and the husband's girlfriend as guests on her show. Unexpectedly, the man announced his girlfriend was pregnant. The pain on the wife's face made Oprah stop, turn to the woman, and say, "I'm really sorry you had to hear this on television. This never should have happened."

She has drawn certain boundaries having to do with dignity and respect for others.

Love is a subject that comes up regularly on her show. Famous people have been known to seek her out to discuss relationship questions and get her input; according

When Oprah was a child, she wanted to grow up to be like Diana Ross (above), one of her idols, and she was frustrated until she came to realize it was okay, perhaps even better, just to be herself.

to rumors these include British princess Diana. Whatever the case, Princess Di invited Oprah to lunch at Kensington Palace in England in April 1994.

Her comments tend to resonate with the truthfulness of someone who has been there. "Love is not supposed to feel bad," she will impress upon her audience. "I was thirty-two years old before I learned this." She admits to some bad years due to man trouble. "Which had a lot to do with how I saw myself. I couldn't do enough for a man because I felt I was never enough. I thought if I were richer or famous or witty or clever or whatever, I would be enough for someone. As I became comfortable with myself, my life, including my love life, improved tremendously."

Racism, evident or insidious, is another burning issue. "What does racism do to your psyche?" she asks, somewhat rhetorically. She has had people on her show who have taken pills to become temporarily black to find out the difference a color nuance makes. She had two black men being made up as whites (lots of makeup and false facial hair) before sending them out into the street to ask for directions. As whites, they were not perceived as a threat, despite looking rather weird, while as black men they frightened several people. "Most people aren't even aware they are exhibiting racist behavior," she noted. She has presented shows to examine self-hatred—once by bringing on a doctor to speak about plastic surgery to make a face look more Caucasian. In ongoing attempts to take away the *fear of life*, she will talk about education and the importance of it, personal finances, health—a wide range of issues.

Serious subjects demonstrate her impressively vast knowledge and straight-to-the-point insights. Content combined with a sense of timing worthy of a stand-up comic results in success as well as relevance.

Her guests are varied—from the waitress in a small restaurant to whom a customer left his estate worth half a million to a woman who received a beautiful home and five cars from Elvis Presley. "Every two, three years he just gave me a new car," revealed a black woman with a mischievous grin. "But what did you do to get it?" exclaimed Oprah with raised eyebrows, and the audience leaned forward, fascinated. It turned out the woman, Mary Jenkins, was the personal cook for the king of rock'n'roll.

"What did he like to eat?" Oprah asked on everyone's behalf. The woman said he liked unusual things, like a fried peanut-butter-and-banana sandwich. His favorite meal? A roast beef dinner with banana pudding for dessert.

Authors who have a chance to go on her show and talk about their books are practically guaranteed a huge increase in sales, beginning instantly.

Pearls of wisdom, cultivated through living and learning, drop naturally from Oprah's lips.

"Life is what you perceive it to be."

"Go with the flow of life. Listen to your instincts."

"Don't fall for the temptation of 'goal overload.'"

"What we do counts; what we fail to do or refuse to do counts sometimes even more."

"Freedom without self-mastery is a delusion."

When she turns toward the camera, opening her swimming-pool-size eyes wide, her hand reaching out in a compelling gesture, and says, *You will be successful!*" there is something almost hypnotic in her stance and voice.

If you have an urge to nod or talk back to your television set, that's exactly what she wants. She aims to get inside her viewers, in order to enable, to empower, to inspire. She believes right will prevail; she also believes in the potential of the so-called "common" man and woman of any age—and in what she calls "divine reciprocity." To her it means: you can get whatever you want but then you have the responsibility to do good with it.

"I want my show to be my voice to the world—my vision of what the world should be."

To that end she has been dramatically retooling, trimming, defining, changing, improving (on her terms) *The Oprah Winfrey Show*. She is confident it will out-last her competition. "Our intentions are better."

So let's take a closer look to find out how talent, a strong spirit, and sheer determination made Oprah rise to the very top from being born black, dirt-poor, and female—the journey of a lonely, abused child with low self-esteem, growing up in our often sexist and racist society. Today she is called "America's most successful woman," and she is a true twentieth-century phenomenon, a powerhouse of mega format whose influence is far-reaching.

Chapter Two

The Name Was Meant To Be "Orpah"

SHE WAS BORN IN the South, with its characteristic climate, landscape, manners and customs, special charm, distinctive rhythm, and a history charged with dramatic and contradictory events—slavery, civil war, and lynchings, as well as explorations, discoveries, and dreams.

Her birth state is Mississippi, admitted as the twentieth state to the Union in 1812. A predominantly rural state, it became a leader in the production of cotton, meaning that slavery flourished. After 1840, slaves outnumbered whites.

Oprah was born in Kosciusko, Mississippi, named for Tadeusz Kosciusko, who came from Poland to fight in the American Revolution. In his will, Kosciusko left money to be used to buy freedom for slaves.

On January 9, 1861, Mississippi was the second state to secede from the Union, and the Civil War hit hard in April 1862. After the war, slavery was abolished but the state government did not adopt a constitution guaranteeing basic rights to African Americans until 1869.

However, in 1874, a black man, A.K. Davis, became lieutenant governor. Two African Americans represented the state of Mississippi in the United States Senate: Hiram Revels for a partial term of 1870-1871, and Blanche Kelso Bruce for a full term of 1875-1881. (Bruce was actually proposed for the vice presidency in 1880 but withdrew; he was eventually appointed registrar of the United States Treasury by President James A. Garfield.)

Always a study in contrasts, Mississippi then bolstered white supremacy in 1890 by passing a law demanding that voters must be able to read and interpret any of the state constitution's provisions. Many black Mississippians could not read. Neither could many whites, but the test was rarely applied to them.

On the ruins of the shattered plantation system rose the sharecropping system, just about guaranteeing lifelong poverty.

Jim Crow laws (legalized segregation)

In the Reconstruction period that followed the Civil War, Mississippi had several black officials. One of the most prominent was Senator Blanche K. Bruce, seen above, who came close to being nominated for the vice presidency in 1880.

were enacted in 1904. In 1948, Mississippi abandoned the Democratic party because of its national stand on civil rights. The 1954 Supreme Court ruling against racial segregation in public schools occasioned massive resistance.

That was the year a certain Oprah Gail Winfrey was born in Mississippi, more precisely in the tiny hamlet of Kosciusko, approximately seventy miles north of the state capital, Jackson.

Kosciusko was named after Tadeusz Kosciuszko, a Polish general who was committed to the cause of liberty to the extent that he traveled to the New World to fight on behalf of those held in slavery. After the war, he went back to his country to fight for Poland's independence but left money in his will to buy freedom for slaves in America.

In the sultry spring of 1953, romance was in Kosciusko's soft, fragrant air, when a twenty-year-old soldier, Vernon Winfrey, met a pretty eighteen-year-old girl named Vernita Lee. He then went back to serving in the army, not knowing that Vernita was pregnant until after baby Oprah was born on January 29, 1954, when the new mother sent him a birth announcement and a note: "Please send clothes."

The baby was meant to be named "Orpah,"

Although the name is misspelled on the sign in this picture, Winfrey Road, which runs between Poplar Creek, Mississippi, and Highway 35, was named for Oprah's ancestors, who had lived along the road since the end of the Civil War.

Winfrey Road is a beautiful wooded country road, about three miles long. Most of the houses along the road were occupied by Winfreys, her father's relatives, when Oprah was a child.

When her home community decided to name a road in her honor—the Oprah Winfrey Road, Oprah went down to Mississippi for the dedication ceremonies.

a name suggested by an aunt who had read it in the Bible, specifically the Book of Ruth, where Orpah is Ruth's sister-in-law. When the name was registered, the letters "r" and "p" were reversed and it came out as "Oprah." So she was an original from the very first, our Oprah, who was mostly called "Gail" during the first years of her existence.

Life wasn't easy for a teenage mother who dreamed of more opportunities than her small hometown offered, especially after the local cotton mill had closed. Vernita left her baby with her own mother, Hattie Mae Lee, who owned a small farm along with her husband, Earless Lee, and she took a Greyhound bus to Milwaukee, Wisconsin. The only job she could find there was as a cleaning lady.

From time to time, she would send for her baby but, with her long working hours and living in the noisy downtown of an industrial city, she was convinced her little one was better off on her grandmother's farm.

The baby grew into a bright, articulate toddler, and her grandmother's friends would nod knowingly. "This girl is gifted, mark my words. She's going somewhere." She might have heard them and been stimulated to keep learning more, doing more, and, as a direct result, getting more praise.

Perhaps she also needed to fight off an ever-present feeling of loneliness. Her grandmother was a good woman but not given to lavish displays of affection. "I would have benefitted from being hugged a lot but she wasn't the kind to do that. It wasn't her fault; it had to do with how she had been brought up," she has said.

Her grandmother, whom she called "Momma," had worked hard her whole life, living without indoor plumbing and other conveniences. Her way of showing love was to keep the girl clean, fed, and with her hair neatly pulled into a multitude of tiny braids.

Oprah's grandfather remained a feared figure in the background, a dark presence to keep away from.

Early on, little Oprah would help care for the few chickens, one cow, and some hogs, as well as do other chores, such as carrying endless pails of water from the well into the house.

It seems her love of an audience had awakened early. She would trot off to the Baptist church at her grandmother's side, they would read the Bible together, and she liked to recite Bible stories—from age three, according to reports. She made those into small dramatic performances, which she practiced on the farm animals, each of

*The church on Winfrey Road where Oprah's grandfather, Rev.
Elmore Winfrey, preached is still there, though it fell into disre-
pair many years ago. As a small child, Oprah was so influenced*

by her grandfather's sermons that she became known for her ability to quote Bible verses. She got attention by showing off her talent to friends, who nicknamed her "Miss Jesus."

whom she had given a name. Thus prepared, she took every opportunity in church to grab the attention she craved. "She's always showing off," other children said, calling her "Miss Jesus" and shunning her company.

When she entered kindergarten, she already knew how to read and write, and she found the lessons silly. Consequently, she sat down and carefully worded a letter to her teacher, explaining she felt she did not belong. Her teacher agreed, and Oprah went straight into first grade. Even among those older children she read better than anyone else.

A good student without a doubt but also endowed with a special talent for getting into trouble in small ways. This was frequently the result of an exuberance that made her break things, spill stuff, and interrupt adults.

The proper punishment for misbehaving, even in minor ways, in many families in the 1950s was a whipping, preferably with the child being sent out to break off suitable twigs or branches. "Spare the rod, spoil the child," it was said and believed. Or "children should be seen not heard," which was difficult to the point of impossibility for this little chatterbox. So the whippings were many

REV. S. H. WINFREY
DEC. 24, 1866
AUG. 20, 1963

The Winfrey Cemetery on Winfrey Road contains the gravestones of her ancestors and close relatives. The marker above is for a Rev. S.H. Winfrey, who was born in 1866 and who died in 1963.

and stinging, which made her look longingly at little white girls with their Shirley Temple curls. She wanted to be one of them because they didn't look as if they were ever whipped. Nor did they have to go through the torture of having their hair tightly braided.

As an adult, she has commented on the practice of whipping children, such as when her talk show has dealt with the issue of corporal punishment in the schools. "My grandmother used to whip my behind, saying 'I do this because I love you' and I'd want to say, 'If you loved me, you'd get that switch off my butt.'"

There was no television in her grandmother's house, but occasionally Oprah would see one show or another when visiting somebody else. She saw white folks with their children and believed real people lived and acted as they did on shows such as *Leave It to Beaver*. This show (which ran from 1957 to 1963) portrayed a close-knit, affectionate family in a small town, centering on the children, two boys. Beaver, who is seven at the beginning of the series, is trusting, friendly, yet still full of mischief. His brother Wally is twelve, uncoordinated, shy, and trying to combine being a "good boy" at home with being cool in the eyes of his peers.

As a child, Oprah watched television sitcoms like Leave It to Beaver *and believed this was the norm for families. Oprah iden-tified with Beaver, the mischievous child of the family.*

In 1960, Oprah was six, and her mother, working as a maid in Milwaukee, decided she wanted her daughter with her. By this time, Vernita had given birth to another girl, Patricia, who was light-skinned. It seemed to Oprah the baby got more attention because of her looks. As the 1960s rolled in, light skin was generally considered prettier than dark skin. So her half-sister was the pretty one, while Oprah was the smart one. Oprah turned to books for companionship, secretly hoping somebody would find her pretty.

She couldn't do anything about her color but perhaps she could make her nose more elegantly thin? She experimented with trying to sleep with a clothespin clamped on her nose—until she gave it up as an exercise in futility.

The family of three lived in a cramped rented apartment on a heavily trafficked street in inner-city Milwaukee, a far cry from the isolated farm life and the wide-open spaces.

At school, Oprah was getting top grades, which can be less than the smoothest road to popularity among less academically gifted or dedicated peers. Her classmates took to calling her "bookworm" and "teacher's pet."

Her mother's long hours as a domestic

paid minimal wages, yet she managed to keep her children clean and well-dressed. "You don't have to look poor because you are," said she, who took great care with her own appearance. For instance, she never wore her maid's uniform on the bus to and from work.

Life was quite lonely, and Oprah wanted desperately a dog to hug and talk to but that was out of the question. Too expensive to keep, her mother said. However, there were plenty of roaches around, and a few years ago she happened to mention in an interview that she would "catch them, put them in a jar, name them, and feed them." Looking over the extensive writing by journalists about her life, it seems her keeping roaches as pets has at times taken precedence over other accomplishments of hers!

Her mother was young but her life consisted mainly of hard work, and with two small children to care for in her minimal "free time," there was little room for entertainment. So when Oprah's father, quite aware of the hardships the young single mother must be going through, suggested that Oprah come to live with him and his wife, Vernita agreed, although reluctantly.

Vernon Winfrey had moved to Nashville, Tennessee, when he got out of the army in

Although the house where her mother lived when Oprah was born is no longer there, some of the Winfrey family farms are still on Winfrey Road, though most are no longer occupied.

The abandoned house in the above photograph taken in the 1980s belonged to one of Oprah's relatives, and it is one of the country places that was familiar to her when she visited family.

1955. He had married a young woman named Zelma and was working two jobs: as janitor at Vanderbilt University and as pot washer at City Hospital. It meant long hours of manual labor, but he had definite goals in sight. He had come from a family with a lot of dignity and pride. A writer from Mississippi remembers hearing about Vernon's father, Oprah's paternal grandfather, who was a preacher of such persuasive powers that many white people used to join his congregation on Sundays, when singing and preaching were offered all day long.

To dig deeper into the Winfrey roots, an investigation (conducted by a *National Enquirer* team in the spring of 1994) reveals that Oprah's great-great-grandfather was Constantine who married to Violet, the two being the only slaves owned by one Absalom Winfrey, a man of modest means. When Constantine and Violet were freed after the Civil War, they moved half a mile away from Winfrey—evidently taking his last name as their own—and raised nine children on their farm. One son, Neinous, Oprah's great-grandfather, became a teacher in an all-black school. He had two sons; one was Elmore Winfrey, the farmer/preacher who fathered Vernon.

The reputation of the several generations

of black Winfreys, according to the report, was that they were hardworking, level-headed, prosperous, and proud.

Vernon and his wife wanted a family and had been deeply disappointed when she had suffered several miscarriages. The decision to take in Oprah had been made jointly, and Zelma was excitedly looking forward to the prospect of having Vernon's child in the house.

So at age eight, it was time for Oprah to pack her few belongings for the third move of her young life.

Living in Nashville was neither like her early years on the farm nor being cooped up in cramped quarters in Milwaukee. Zelma, like Vernon, was a strong believer in education and was appalled to find that Oprah, although an excellent reader, did not know her multiplication tables. A rigid home study schedule was made up with frequent drillings on vocabulary and other skills. Outside of her regular school work, Oprah was required to read a book a week and report on it. Although the demands were hard, the child sensed it was good for her.

Zelma and Vernon were active in Faith United Church, and Oprah went with them with increasing religious zeal. Her third-grade teacher let her lead devotion on

Mondays. Would she perhaps become a preacher? She began to fantasize about going to some faraway, exotic place as a missionary. Already ideas and action were close allies in her mind; she began collecting money for starving kids in Costa Rica and turned every penny over to a missionary fund.

Oprah sailed into fourth grade, taught by a Mrs. Dunkin. She idolized her teacher. Perhaps she would become a fourth-grade teacher?

She was pleased with her life and had made a few friends when she was told she was going back to Milwaukee for the summer. Her mother missed her and had talked Vernon into letting Oprah visit. Vernita had by now given birth to her third child, a boy, and said she and the boy's father were talking seriously of marriage. She felt she would then be as able as Vernon and his wife to provide her children, including Oprah, with a stable home life.

Vernon and Zelma found the house empty without Oprah and were impatiently looking forward to her return, but when Vernon went to pick up his daughter at summer's end, Oprah's spirits were so low he barely recognized her.

Vernita greeted him with the unwelcome

news that Oprah was staying on. He had no legal rights, so there was nothing he could do.

No longer was Oprah required to read a book a week and report on it. Her mother's marriage never became a reality; she kept working hard and Oprah had to help with her younger siblings. She did not seem to have made close friends at school but remained a loner. She read a lot of books and watched television, mostly programs such as *Leave It to Beaver*, *I Love Lucy*, and *The Andy Griffith Show*. But she also saw Diana Ross and the Supremes on *The Ed Sullivan Show*—possibly the first time she saw gorgeous, successful black women on the small flickering screen that dominated their home.

Relatives came and went. When her mother worked late, Oprah was sometimes dropped off at someone's apartment for the night, and so it happened that a nineteen-year-old male relative, supposed to babysit, raped her. The next day he took her to the zoo, bought her ice-cream, and warned her of the dire consequences if she ever told anyone. She was nine.

At school, a classmate happened to inform her of the facts of life, including how babies were made. Horror entered her days. Would this happen to her? What would she do? Shame and guilt darkened her life and dampened her spirits.

Her mother kept working long hours, and Oprah was frequently left with male relatives or her mother's boyfriend. She did not dare to protest or tell anyone when they fondled her and did things she knew were wrong. She kept living with her shame, thinking what was happening was all her fault. She had entered the shadowy world of the abused child, a peculiar prison where a child will spend years—sometimes a whole life—punishing herself (or himself) for a crime she or he has never committed.

School was a safer place than home and she was doing excellent work there.

When she was thirteen, a teacher at Lincoln Middle School, Gene Abrahams, recognized her intellectual capacity and obtained a full scholarship for her to attend Nicolet, an exclusive private high school in a wealthy suburb of Milwaukee, more than twenty miles from her mother's apartment. Most of her teachers seemed to have believed she would follow in their footsteps and become a teacher herself. In a way, she has.

On the long bus ride to and from school, Oprah found herself squeezed in between

One of Oprah's favorite television shows as a child was I Love Lucy. *Interestingly, there was to be some similarity between Lucy, the first woman to own her own TV production company, and Oprah, the first black woman to do so.*

women who worked as maids for her school-mates' parents. They were like her mother. Her mother was not like the mothers of her classmates. She did not live like them nor did she buy the things their mothers did. She was not there for Oprah when school was out. She left in the morning and returned late at night, usually exhausted.

Seeing a totally different way of life around her, Oprah translated it into meaning that her mother didn't care like those white mothers. That a poor, single mother's only way to show her caring might be to work unceasingly from morning to night, a child cannot always be expected to understand.

Oprah was the only black student at her new school, but this became a strange kind of advantage rather than a problem. She was seen as an exotic oddity, and the upper-middle-class white girls, who had been touched by the civil-rights movement and the idea of revolution of the 1960s, tried in their well-meaning albeit often clumsy way to show their good intentions and lack of racism. They invited her to their homes, played records with black artists for her, and introduced her to their black servants.

Observing opulent life-styles, designer clothes, and fancy homes, Oprah was

It was on the Ed Sullivan Show *that Oprah first saw successful black women on television, when Sullivan featured Diana Ross and the Supremes. Oprah was so impressed with Diana that she wanted to be like her when she grew up.*

increasingly resenting the dreariness of her home and her life. Calling upon her vivid imagination, she entertained her friends with made-up fanciful stories about how she lived. She took money from her mother's purse to keep up a social life with her class-mates to some extent. Just going for pizza could create a problem for her since her allowance was a fraction of theirs. She began staying out late.

Still a child, she was brimming over with angry frustration and didn't know what to do with it or with herself. A few incidents have been reported, showing a definite the-atricality in her behavior. Once she wanted a certain pair of stylish eyeglasses but couldn't get them, so she staged a break-in, messed up her mother's apartment, and told the police she had been hit in the head, with the result that her old unfashionable but-terfly-rimmed eyeglasses, chosen by her mother over her protests, were broken. She went even further, claiming amnesia, acting it out so well that almost everybody believed her. Not her mother, however.

She had managed to buy a puppy with patiently saved-up nickels and dimes. Then she was told she would not be allowed to keep it because the high-spirited mutt showed no signs of being housebroken.

One one occasion when Oprah ran away from home as a child, she met Aretha Franklin and gave the star a sob story about needing money. The generous Aretha gave her a hundred dollars.

What did she do? She staged a burglary attempt, claiming her dog had foiled the burglars at the last minute!

Although her mother saw right through Oprah's wild yarns, she didn't know how to handle this unpredictable youngster.

The proverbial straw that broke the camel's back was her running away from home. The story goes that she had planned to stay with a girlfriend but failed to inform her friend of her plans. Consequently, she got to her friend's place and nobody was at home. On the street, she happened to spot Aretha Franklin, the Queen of Soul, exiting a limousine. Oprah hurried over to her, sobbing pitifully, saying she had been abandoned and had no money to get back to her home in Ohio. Why Ohio? She liked the sound of it—oh-hi-oh.

The kind singer gave her a hundred dollars, and Oprah promptly rented a hotel room for a week or until her money ran out.

Her inborn acting talent seems to have evidenced itself in rather unorthodox and dramatic ways.

Feeling unable to cope with spirited rebellion at every turn, her mother called Oprah's father and arranged for Oprah to go to live permanently with him and his wife in Nashville.

When the adult Oprah talks about her mother, it is with a great deal of love and understanding. "Like most everybody's mother, she did the best she could, the best she knew how to do."

Vernon (who by this time was a member of the city council) and Zelma Winfrey were delighted to take over as parents. They loved Oprah and saw her potential to accomplish things. The young girl's short skirts and unskillfully applied makeup when she arrived told them the story of how she, feeling lost and confused, had tried to fit in.

Chapter Three

A Teenager in Nashville

OPRAH BEHAVED QUITE differently when living with her father and his wife. They gave her a lot of attention and taught her by example, not by telling her what to do while their day-to-day life told a different story.

She was fourteen, which was the year when another calamity struck, one that might better have been left as part of her private life, shielded from public view. But her half-sister, Patricia, broke the story to a tabloid after Oprah was famous, thereby illustrating how fame shines a search light

During her childhood, Oprah was often shuttled back and forth between her mother's home in Milwaukee (seen at left) and her father's in Nashville, the home that she preferred and was allowed to remain in throughout her high school years.

into every corner of someone's life. In brief, Oprah had gotten pregnant in Milwaukee and gave premature birth to a stillborn baby boy. It was a hard thing for her to handle emotionally but Zelma and Vernon surrounded her with steadfast love without coddling her.

Her father's long hours of work as janitor and pot washer ("the worst job in Nashville") had paid off. He had saved his money and by now owned a barbershop; later he would buy the small grocery store next door. He was a deacon at church, and Oprah went back to religion and an orderly life.

"He was a stern disciplinarian.... It's because of him I'm where I am today," Oprah has said. Yes, it was a life of rules and discipline—and she was mature enough to see these as genuine expressions of love, of caring, of helping her toward a good life.

Again, education was strongly emphasized; reading, the mainstay of education, was a requisite and has remained one of her greatest pleasures. Among the many books Oprah devoured, one made an indelible impression on her: Maya Angelou's *I Know Why the Caged Bird Sings*. It opened a door of discovery into her heritage as a black woman.

The book is an autobiography from child-

Above is the country store at the crossroads town of Poplar Creek, Mississippi, a place that was familiar to Oprah as a child, being the nearest grocery store to her grandparents' farm.

hood to motherhood (at age sixteen), which the author had begun in order to tell black girls something about what it's like to grow up. Of course, as she kept writing, she realized she was writing for an audience that included just about everyone "from middle-aged Chinese women to young Jewish boys with braces on their teeth; really, for anyone in a cage."

Maya Angelou was the first black woman screenwriter; she wrote *Georgia, Georgia* about a black woman singer and her involvement with a young white defector in Sweden. The film was released in 1972. She went on to become a director—one writer calls her a "one-woman creativity cult"—singer, dancer, teacher, poet, author, actress, editor, songwriter, playwright, political activist—and an inspiration to so many who have gone against the odds and answered "you can't do that!" with "you wanna bet?!"

Reading this woman's writing was a revelation to young Oprah. Later on, she and Ms. Angelou would become so close that the latter today tends to refer to Oprah as her spiritual daughter. Certainly they have a lot in common, both their intelligence and an uncertain childhood of hardship and sexual abuse. (In Maya Angelou's case, it resulted in her stopping to speak altogether for a long

The multi-talented Maya Angelou, seen here when she was work-ing as a dancer in Hollywood, was one of Oprah's idols when she was in high school and college. Later the two would become good friends, with Maya calling Oprah her "spiritual daughter."

period of time.) Both women have taken everything that has happened to them—the pain, the mistakes, whatever—and used it to lead lives of immense creativity.

As the 1960s were drawing to a close, Oprah was a rather well-adjusted teenager in Nashville, the center of country music with the Grand Ole Opry and Opryland, eight universities, and Greek-inspired architecture (including a replica of the Parthenon built in 1897).

She was one of the first black students to attend the formerly all-white East High School, one of the earliest schools in Nashville to follow the Supreme Court's mandate of integration. The school offered a vastly different experience from her earlier sojourn at Nicolet in Milwaukee: it was situated in a lower-middle-class neighborhood, and no huge gap existed between her home and life-style and those of her classmates.

She brought home passing grades and was told in no uncertain terms by Zelma and Vernon that passing was not good enough. She had to get used to doing her best; she had to believe she could be more, much more, than she was. They pointed out that, being a kind of pioneer in the era of forced school desegregation, she had a respon-

sibility toward other black youths everywhere and must not feed any stereotypical
images in the minds of anyone.

She listened, understood, and responded
wholeheartedly to the call for excellence.
She knew she could do it. Part of her
immense frustration at Nicolet, resulting in
explosions of revolt, had been that she had
done better in school than those girls
around her who seemed to have everything.
And yet she remained poor. She had nothing of material wealth compared to them.

Her father's philosophy, he informed her,
was that there are three kinds of people:
those who make things happen, those who
watch things happen, and those who are
never sure what is happening.

On the wall of his barbershop he had post-
ed a message to young people:

Attention Teenagers. If you are tired of
being hassled by your parents, now is the
time for action. Leave home and pay your
own way while you still know everything.

Definite hours were set aside for Oprah
to study each day. Television watching was
monitored and held to a minimum. She
began to use her allotted time to watch news
broadcasts.

Oprah's life had been transformed into

one of constant learning, and her grades improved dramatically, as did her verbal skills. She became an honor student.

At age fifteen, she visited California on an excursion from her church, at which time she spoke to California church groups between visiting tourist attractions such as the Grauman's Chinese Theater with its famous footprints of movie stars. One wonders if the world of show business and celebrity seemed light-years away from her reality.

At school Oprah was active in drama classes and student politics. After a zesty campaign, she was elected student body president. In her campaign she did not touch upon racial issues but concentrated on what concerned every student: better food in the cafeteria, improving the school spirit, having live music at the prom, and so on. "Vote for Grand Ole Oprah!" the handmade posters proclaimed.

At age sixteen, she was voted most popular girl in her class. She was thriving, her earlier confusion having disappeared in her new life with a purpose. She had a boyfriend, Anthony, another honor student, who was voted most popular boy. Their relationship was fun and innocent; she had no problems following the strict rules set by her father and the church. She complied easily with the eleven o'clock curfew at night—except perhaps the evening they went to a Jackson Five concert. She couldn't stop talking about the concert and especially about Michael for weeks afterwards, not knowing that one day she would know Michael Jackson very well, and he would express his admiration and affection for her.

In 1970, Oprah was invited to represent East High School at a White House Conference of Youth in Estes Park, Colorado, where five hundred business leaders met with youth from all over the country. She also represented East High as Outstanding Teenager of America, chosen for the honor both for her academic achievement and community service.

Win followed upon win as a result of her being uniquely articulate. She won first place in the Tennessee District of the National Forensic League Tournament for her dramatic reading from Margaret Walker's *Jubilee*. (Poet/writer Margaret Walker, born 1915 in Alabama, wrote the famous poem "For My People" as well as several books; her most famous novel is *Jubilee,* about a slave woman after the Civil War.) Oprah flew to Palo Alto, California, to compete with students from across the country. In June 1970 she won the Tennessee Elks Club oratorial contest.

She was attractive, meaning not just pretty but with an irresistible personality. In 1971, she competed in her first beauty contest, the Miss Fire Prevention contest. When she was interviewed, she had planned to say what she believed to be true—or perhaps she had talked herself into believing this—namely that she wanted to become an elementary school teacher. Instead she heard herself saying: "I believe in truth and I want to perpetuate truth. So I want to be a journalist."

She became one of the three finalists. "What would you do if you had a million dollars?" was the question asked of each one. One girl declared she would provide for members of her family, the other that she would give to the poor, and then it was Oprah's turn. "I'd be a spending fool!" The honest exclamation drew smiles on the faces of the judges.

Right there might lie one of the secrets behind her success—she simply tells the truth. It explains why she is at ease with any question, in just about any situation. She does not get entangled in a web of lies or rationalizations or in frantically trying to impress. "Politically correct" or not, Oprah tends to speak her mind with a great deal of spontaneity.

She won—the first black girl to do so. Again, she was pretty enough with her big eyes and even bigger smile but perhaps not stunningly beautiful according to generally accepted standards of the time. Her victory must be attributed in no small part to her effervescence, her poise, her ability to *make people see her as she wanted to be seen.* Another Oprah success secret.

She went to collect her prizes—a watch and a digital clock—and one of the sponsoring radio station's disc jockeys, a man named John Heidelberg, happened to stop by. Impressed by her confidence, her ability to enunciate, and the quality of her voice, he asked if she had ever considered a career in broadcasting. He handed her a page of news copy and asked her to read it.

She did. ("Basically, I was pretending to be a newscaster.") He put her on tape and let the radio station manager hear it. The manager of the station, WVOL (black-operated but white-owned, and most of its listeners were black), was impressed by her rich voice and her manner of reading but hesitated. After all, she was only a girl of seventeen. However, after a considerable amount of discussion for and against, she got a part-time job as news announcer, working at the station after school, reading the news every half hour until 8:30 P.M. Her father was skeptical at first but was assured that his daughter would neither be mistreated nor led astray.

She was delighted, of course—not the least because it took her out of working weekends in her father's small grocery store. At the station everyone was pleased, especially as there was pressure put upon them to employ more members of minorities as well as more women; in her person they had gotten two for one (what was called a "twofer"). If it had not been for the (by FCC required) affirmative action program, chances are that Oprah, if she had been employed at all, would have been relegated to reading household hints rather than news, which for a long time was reserved exclusively for male radio voices.

After a training period with no salary, she was paid a hundred dollars a week. Although she made some mistakes here and there, she was generally well received. At the same time, she excelled at school and found time to be on the committee to arrange and plan the prom, with the theme "Evening above the Clouds." Interestingly, the motto of her senior class was: "We've

Only Just Begun."

She entered and won the Miss Black Nashville contest in March 1972. Her prize was a four-year scholarship to Tennessee State University (TSU) right there in Nashville. Her father was pleased because she could keep on living at home, though *she* would actually have preferred to go away to college and be on her own.

She graduated from high school in June 1972. As Miss Black Nashville, she competed against six other contestants in the Miss Black Tennessee pageant later that month—and won that one too, to the astonishment of the other contestants and even herself.

She was especially surprised because she had been the darkest girl of them all, and her whole life she had believed that light was prettier than dark. This was at a time when "dark" was not often paired with "lovely" so, because her skin was fudge rather than milk chocolate, she felt she had to be the best and the smartest to make up for it.

In August, she was given an all-expense-paid trip to Hollywood to compete in the Miss Black America pageant. By now, she might have been growing tired of beauty contests. She had proven something to herself—so why stand there like a prize calf and turn this way and that for a panel of judges, for them to assess and compare, still with a great deal of emphasis on physical qualities? She did what she had done before, meaning she focused on her poise and talent, choosing rather plain clothes, while other contestants paid more attention to swimsuits and evening gowns.

For the talent portion, she had decided on a monologue that would include the spiritual "Sometimes I Feel Like a Motherless Child." She would enter dressed as an old woman with black tights and a black, long-sleeved leotard underneath and was supposed to shed the outer layer during her routine.

However, when her turn came, she did not do what she had told her sponsors she would. For her performance, she appeared in the old-woman clothing, a bandanna wrapped around her head, and never removed any part of her costume; for the parade she wore a frilly gown instead of the sophisticated one chosen for her. Did she subtly sabotage her chances of winning? If so, she succeeded. She did not make it as a finalist. While other girls who had not made it were crying, Oprah seemed jubilant. When it was over, she happily donned the flattering gown she had been supposed to wear during the parade.

When her father heard about this, he laughed approvingly. "Oprah makes her own decisions," he said proudly.

She started at TSU in September 1972, as a speech and drama major, while continuing her part-time job as a newscaster.

Surprisingly enough, she did not take to college. Perhaps one reason was the circumstance of having to continue living at home and commute the seven miles every day.

Or was it the racial climate? The social changes initiated in the 1960s were slow in coming into fruition, and there were various racial controversies on many college campuses. Tennessee State University was all-black. African studies were part of the curriculum. Political demonstrations were held regularly.

Oprah Winfrey watched and reflected. She acknowledged those who had gone before her, especially the women—Sojourner Truth, the former slave who became a voice for her people, Fannie Lou Hamer, the brave civil rights activist, Madam C. J. Walker, the businesswoman and philanthropist. But there were ways in which she did not agree with the speech-making activists on campus. A belief deep inside her insisted that

As Oprah matured she learned about many of the successful black women who had preceded her, among them the famed Madam C.J. Walker, seen above driving one of her automobiles.

Madam Walker was one of the first African-American entrepreneurs, creating a line of beauty products especially formulated for the skin and hair of black women.

excellence was the best deterrent to racism and sexism, that the best argument for anyone's equal rights was "to be the best you can ever be."

She could not quite identify with the hostility expressed by many of her peers. "It was *in* to be angry," she has commented. She questioned whether hatred and blame, however well-deserved, accomplished anything real. She felt she had already tested and proven that sheer ability and iron-willed determination could get her what she wanted. Being an avid reader, perhaps she had come across the philosophers who maintain that the highest activity "is an effect rather than an act."

She felt an outsider, a feeling all too familiar from her childhood. She was criticized for what was seen as her unwillingness to take an active part in the causes. She was called an "Oreo" (black on the outside, white on the inside), which hurt, but she couldn't see hating someone just for being white. Color didn't matter to her; only who a person was all the way through. She was striving to become the kind of human being who would radiate positive energy and thereby do her bit to change the world to a better place. She didn't feel others understood exactly what she was about, and sometimes

James Weldon Johnson, one of the great African-American writers of the Harlem Renaissance, was the author of God's Trombones, *a play that Oprah used to create a one-woman show for herself during her years at Tennessee State University.*

she was not absolutely sure herself.

Her self-esteem went down as her old feelings of loneliness and uncertainty took hold of her. It would have been easier to join, to follow the herd, but this was not—and never would be—her style.

Add to this that her romantic life was far from satisfactory. She had fallen hard—as she was wont to do—for a young man named William. She had even made the radio station hire him, although he didn't quite cut it and went on to become a mortician. Believing herself to be madly in love with him for all eternity, she was desperately unhappy when he left. Of course, she was unable to look into her future and realize how relieved and happy she would be one day that she had not ended up as part of his life.

The failed romance and her feeling of isolation resulted in her throwing herself even more intensely into her studies and her work at the radio station. She even found time to participate in the drama department's projects. Appreciating her talents fully was the late Dr. Thomas E. Poag, who had won fame as being the first black person to receive a master's degree and a PhD in Theater Arts in the United States. He had founded TSU's speech and theater department and could easily imagine this young lady as a full-time actress.

At TSU, she played the role of Coretta Scott King in a student-written play about Dr. Martin Luther King. She performed dramatic readings from plays. Just about every Sunday she did readings in the area's churches from *God's Trombone* by James Weldon Johnson. It became a one-woman show, in which she was accompanied by the group Sweet Honey in the Rock. She participated in a drama conference in Chicago and won second place for her dramatic reading of Ntozake Shange's *For Colored Girls Who Have Considered Suicide When the Rainbow Is Enuf*.

Chapter Four

What is An Oprah?

OPRAH'S LIFE WAS about to change. The television network CBS had an affiliate in Nashville, WTVF (Channel 5), and suddenly she received an offer to audition for the position of television newscaster.

She became unbearably nervous. Not only her voice but all of her would be out there to be scrutinized, judged, criticized. She had frequently watched Barbara Walters doing her television interviews and had nurtured secret fantasies about having a show like hers. Consequently she went to the audition, trying to pretend she was Ms. Walters,

Oprah's broadcasting career began while she was still in college. Her first job was as a radio newscaster in Nashville; then in 1973, she became news co-anchor on WTVF-TV, moving on to station WJZ-TV in Baltimore in 1976.

with crossed ankles, little finger under her chin and all.

She landed the position.

Later, when she told Barbara Walters about this, Walters exclaimed, "Thank goodness you got the job!"

Someone who worked at the station back then says she did not come across as Barbara Walters but as Oprah Winfrey. Especially impressive was her unique combination of being simultaneously calmly authoritative and warmly friendly. She became the weekend news anchor.

Would she now have to give up college and her radio work?

The radio job had to go, but she found it impossible to continue attending college while working in television. And she still lived at home with her parents, thereby becoming probably the only news anchor anywhere who had to be home by midnight!

Oprah was Nashville's first anchorwoman and first black anchorperson.

She thrived on every challenge. There was no producer for the weekend news so she and her co-anchor, Harry Chapman, had to decide on which stories to report as well as to write the scripts for them. Often they would go out as reporters, tape stories, write and edit them—and present them on the air.

Her one drawback might have been her tendency to become too emotionally involved in some of her interviews. If a tragedy had struck a family, she would cry with them and give them money from her own pocket.

In front of the camera, she was remarkably relaxed and comfortable. Viewers responded well to her.

With calm logic she realized that part of the positive response from everyone she worked with was the fact that, in the reigning political climate, the station needed to fill its quota and she was the "token black," but, as she said at one time, "I was a happy, paid token!"

She was twenty-two years old, and her need to live on her own was growing stronger. As long as she worked in Nashville, however—and her job was immensely important to her—it was difficult to pack up and move away from home.

Soon enough, life took care of this matter for her, as so often before and after.

Unbeknownst to her, the folks at a Baltimore station had been watching her for months, and again an offer came her way— for the job as co-anchor for their evening news. The station, WJZ-TV in Baltimore, the state of Maryland's metropolis, with a population of almost a million, was the tenth largest market in the nation, double that of Nashville. She jumped at the chance and packed her bags, feeling excited about this major life change.

She arrived in Baltimore in June 1976, finding big posters with the words "WHAT IS AN OPRAH?" as part of the publicity campaign to draw viewers. She would be the station's first female co-anchor. Her partner was a male veteran, Jerry Turner. He was well-known but she was of course a total stranger to the audience. So the promotion campaign, centering on her unusual name, had been invented by the station.

For whatever reason, there was no spark between her and Turner. For the first time, she felt stiff and formal on the air—or else she fell into the trap of being too emotionally involved in stories she was reporting. There were complaints. She was told to speak and behave with an objective attitude and to avoid expressing her own feelings.

Her looks were criticized too. Her chin was too big, her features were all wrong. She was sent to a "specialist" who was supposed to dress her more attractively and to an expensive hair designer to have her hair styled differently. He gave her what he called a French perm—and her hair fell out! "Just three little squiggles in front, otherwise I was bald. I looked like Kojak," she told viewers during a recent show that focused on beauty emergencies.

To complicate matters further, Oprah has a large head and couldn't find a wig to fit her. She had to resort to wearing artfully tied scarves around her head—not exactly the thing to make her feel good and gorgeous in front of television cameras.

The so-called "improvement" procedure continued. The station sent her to a speech coach in New York, who thought she was too friendly and familiar on the air and advised her to toughen up.

She felt pulled in different directions, which was not a happy state. Confused and dejected, she presented a striking contrast to the bubbly, energetic, friendly Oprah in Nashville. Would her big adventure and promising career end in resounding failure?

Then a change in management took place at the station, and the new manager wanted to re-style their regular morning show to compete with the nation's number-one talk show, hosted by stupendously popular Phil Donahue. Seeing something special in Oprah, the manager wanted her to be part of this show. At first she resisted, feeling a morning show was a step down from doing the news and suspecting it to be the first stage in the station's plan to get rid of her.

In the end, she agreed to do it. For one thing, she didn't have much of a choice.

The morning show, dubbed *People Are Talking*, went on the air in 1977. Oprah was co-hosting with Richard Sher, an experienced broadcaster in Baltimore. Lo and behold, the two of them clicked from the very first.

As guests on their initial show, they had the cast of ABC's daytime soap *All My Children*, and Oprah found herself having a really good time.

There was a tingle inside as if every cell in her body, every nerve ending, told her: This is it, girl! You've come home! You're good at this and it's good for you—consequently it's good for those who are watching.

She had found her niche.

"It's like breathing," said this born communicator jubilantly, and she kept working hard on the shows. She found no contradiction in working intensely on something that came naturally, because she knew only hard, detailed work makes everything flow and seem easy.

The show became a nearly instant hit in Baltimore, and it accomplished what some had considered impossible: it outdid the

Her normal confidence and sunny nature took a backseat. She ended up in a dark pit of despair, the place where you see no solution, no hope, no light at the end of the tunnel, and, having missed work on September 8, 1981, she decided to end it all. She put her papers in order, asked a friend to water her plants, and even formulated a suicide note. She was twenty-seven years old, admired by many and making good money, but her love life was nil and her accomplishments felt echoingly empty without somebody to share her life.

Obviously, she never carried out her plan. Her own personality stopped her. With her blend of deep-seated optimism and never-ending curiosity, there was no way for her to check out.

She learned an important lesson from this. In her shows, she has talked about people who are victims of emotional abuse, referring to those who stay in relationships that clip their wings, preventing them from being all they could be.

"I will never—as long as I'm black—give up my power to another person again," she vowed.

After seven years of constant learning, of honing her skills in every way, of sensing what viewers would really want to know to

a degree no other talk-sho truly listening to people, of h audience, she wanted to exp further. She wanted to untried; she wanted yet ar she wanted to act.

She got a small part on th *My Children* (in 1983)—ar times her salary on three she needed only one for he with just a few brief lines scene. She had an absolute

By now, her producer, De left Baltimore for Chicago producing *A.M. Chicago*, popular talk show. The 1 show had been Steve Edv warm approach to the job ; ratings during his three ; lowed by a couple of oth five years, during which t had moved in and ta Temporary celebrity host but something essential show, something necessai first-rate status.

DiMaio, who knew Op could do, wanted her to suggested this to the ma Oprah appreciated DiM

her b
get th
that h
politi
gettir
Washi

She
ning tl
looking
They 1
might
givings

"You
the ma

"We
want t

Winr
midabl
pheno
watche
this bla
go up
match,

The 1
all, Dor
talk sho
they w
probabl
Later i
wrong, l

Donahue show in the local market. Before long, the show was syndicated in twelve other cities.

Professional success was persistently increasing the next few years but personally things were going less well for Oprah. A steady boyfriend, a television reporter, moved to New York, and she was lonely. Like many lonely people, she turned to food for comfort.

Her loneliness drove her also into an unhealthy relationship with a man who was wrong for her. She has referred to this in her shows and to the fact that many women of all ages feel they are worthless without a man in their life, forgetting that self-worth originates in one's own self.

She remained in a relationship that should never have been and which kept getting increasingly destructive, probably feeling anything was better than being all alone. When the man began to reject her, she wanted him even more.

The danger with lack of self-esteem, she frequently points out to guests on her show, is that when you feel bad about yourself and somebody else tells you in words and actions that they consider you no good, you tend not only to agree with them but think they really see and understand you!

Her normal confidence and sunny nature took a backseat. She ended up in a dark pit of despair, the place where you see no solution, no hope, no light at the end of the tunnel, and, having missed work on September 8, 1981, she decided to end it all. She put her papers in order, asked a friend to water her plants, and even formulated a suicide note. She was twenty-seven years old, admired by many and making good money, but her love life was nil and her accomplishments felt echoingly empty without somebody to share her life.

Obviously, she never carried out her plan. Her own personality stopped her. With her blend of deep-seated optimism and never-ending curiosity, there was no way for her to check out.

She learned an important lesson from this. In her shows, she has talked about people who are victims of emotional abuse, referring to those who stay in relationships that clip their wings, preventing them from being all they could be.

"I will never—as long as I'm black—give up my power to another person again," she vowed.

After seven years of constant learning, of honing her skills in every way, of sensing what viewers would really want to know to a degree no other talk-show hosts did, of truly listening to people, of bonding with her audience, she wanted to expand her horizon further. She wanted to try something untried; she wanted yet another challenge: she wanted to act.

She got a small part on the soap opera *All My Children* (in 1983)—and spent several times her salary on three outfits although she needed only one for her one day's work with just a few brief lines in a restaurant scene. She had an absolutely fabulous time.

By now, her producer, Debbie DiMaio, had left Baltimore for Chicago, where she was producing *A.M. Chicago*, the Windy City's popular talk show. The first host for the show had been Steve Edwards, who had a warm approach to the job and pulled in good ratings during his three years. He was followed by a couple of other hosts the next five years, during which the *Donahue* show had moved in and taken first place. Temporary celebrity hosts had been tried, but something essential was lacking in the show, something necessary for it to achieve first-rate status.

DiMaio, who knew Oprah and what she could do, wanted her to host the show. She suggested this to the management.

Oprah appreciated DiMaio's confidence in

her but did not believe it likely she would get the job. One reason was the racial strife that had erupted in the city during a bitter political campaign, resulting in Chicago getting its first black mayor, Harold Washington.

She was not aware that the people running the station, WLS-TV, had already been looking with fascination in her direction. They knew they wanted her, even if there might have been some who expressed misgivings.

"You realize I'm black," Oprah said when the manager called her.

"We don't care what color you are—we want to win," he told her straightforwardly.

Winning meant competing with the formidable Phil Donahue, a true talk-show phenomenon, loved and trusted and watched by millions and millions. How could this black—and by now overweight—female go up against all he offered? An uneven match, it would seem.

The pessimists pointed out that, first of all, Donahue was invincible and, secondly, talk shows had worn out the novelty factor; they were beginning to falter, and would probably soon lose their appeal altogether. Later it would be clear that they were wrong, but nobody had a reliable crystal ball for peeks into the future. Actually, no one—except Oprah, Debbie DiMaio, and one or two friends—really believed it possible for her to come, talk, and conquer Chicago.

"I'll do my best," said Oprah with a glint in her eye, stimulated by the difficulty that in her vocabulary tends to mean challenge. She packed her bags, signed a four-year contract at a reported yearly salary of $200,000, and landed in Chicago on a December day in 1983—in the middle of a severe cold spell with a wind like a double-bladed knife.

Another big change in her life and career. As she stepped off the plane, was she nervous? Apprehensive? Anxious? Or more excited than anything else?

We might surmise that there was a dose of anxiety and that she sought solace in food. After her long workdays, solitude awaited her. She had no close friends in Chicago and spent her first Christmas working in a soup kitchen.

On her first New Year's Eve she wasn't alone, however; she spent it with a lot of people because she was given the assignment to provide live coverage of Chicago's State Street celebrations.

Although she knew practically no one, practically everyone in the city seemed to know and love her almost instantly. After one month, her thirty-minute show, *A.M. Chicago*, had achieved its highest rating in years. Within twelve weeks, talk-show king Phil Donahue was eased off his throne and relegated to second place. Oprah was number one in Chicago!

Part of her success was due to her producers being wise enough to give her relatively free reign. Although carefully scripted questions for guests were handed to her, more often than not she would veer away from the written words and just ask whatever she was curious to know. She didn't want to ask questions for which she already knew the answers—because she was turned off by anything that seemed fake or artificial. She had an uncanny ability for coming up with the very questions the viewers at home wanted to ask.

The show was relaxed, fun, comfortable, and informative. People loved this woman who seemed fearless and unpredictable enough to keep them glued to the small screen.

One of the first guests on her show was Paul McCartney, and her audience identified totally when she told him how she, as a teenager, had kept her bedroom walls plastered with Beatles posters. She followed this confession by asking him in a banter-

When Oprah began her thirty-minute talk show, A.M. Chicago, one of her early celebrity guests was singer Stevie Wonder, seen here in a publicity photo taken for an NBC special honoring Dr. Martin Luther King, Jr., in 1986.

ing manner if he used to think of her too!

Other early celebrity guests were Stevie Wonder, Shirley MacLaine, Billy Dee Williams, Tom Selleck, Candice Bergen, Dudley Moore ("I'd marry that man tomorrow—he's so naturally funny!"), Goldie Hawn, as well as Barbara Walters and Maya Angelou, her two role models, although for widely different reasons. When she did those two interviews, a sharp-eyed viewer might have noticed that she was a little less relaxed. Was it possible that she was just a tiny bit intimidated?

Speaking of Barbara Walters, at one time the *Washington Post* compared her and Oprah. "People want to hold Barbara Walters' hand. They want to crawl into Winfrey's lap," they wrote, acknowledging the warmth she exudes.

The producers requested controversial, emotional topics and true-life stories. Oprah complied. Viewers were encouraged to call in and ask questions, and Oprah made everything seem totally spontaneous, which meant that each show was preceded by considerable research and deliberation.

Not only is Oprah Winfrey a woman with a rare kind of intuition and sensitivity; with her background, she and her guests could always find some common ground. "Everybody has felt victimized at some point in their lives, be it during a hard childhood or during their adulthood. The question is—where do we go from there?"

She had female members of the Ku Klux Klan on her show, and many viewers were amazed seeing her so calm in the face of their blatant racism. Oprah just smiled. She knew who she was. "When the show is over, those people are still gonna be the Klan and I'm still gonna be Oprah." By having them and people like them on her show, she felt she had a chance to expose racism as the combination of stupidity, ignorance, and fear that it is.

After seven months, her show was expanded to sixty minutes. At the end of her first year, *Newsweek* magazine published a long article about her.

She appeared on Johnny Carson's *Tonight* show for the first time on her thirty-first birthday (January 29, 1985), with Joan Rivers as guest host. The two ladies exchanged quips and entered into a weight-losing contest. Later Oprah appeared with Joan Rivers on *The Late Show*, and again their conversation touched on diets. Oprah claimed she has been on every diet invented. Many viewers felt closer to her because of her weight problem; although she seemed to have everything, there was one flaw for all to see. (At least it tends to be perceived as a flaw in a society where slimness has been overemphasized and overvalued.) Some guests on her show expressed their feelings strongly: "Please, don't lose one pound. Don't! We love you exactly as you are."

In September 1985, the name of her show was changed to *The Oprah Winfrey Show*.

No subject frightened her off, whether it was about hating your boss/parents/siblings or cheating on exams or being fat or wondering about sexual problems or whatever.

Her strong sympathy and compassion for child-abuse victims were expressed in no uncertain terms, followed by her revelation on one show that she had been abused as a child. As the guests on the show spoke of their experiences, revealing the emotional pain and trauma they had suffered, she reacted spontaneously. "I know—it happened to me!" The audience gasped. Afterward, she worriedly asked herself if she had made a mistake but was to find out differently as the reaction from viewers was potent, emotional, and admiring. Many verbalized their gratitude to her for having the courage to discuss publicly a subject that had been taboo for too long.

"People everywhere congratulated me," she said later. "And for me it was good therapy, a catharsis. I no longer had to live with this horrible secret, and I knew it could help others who had suffered the same way."

As a thread through her perfectly orchestrated shows, in which she treated studio audiences as friends and neighbors with whom she felt free to share experiences and listen to whatever concerned them, ran her emphatic message to all, in the studio or watching in their homes: they could and should regain control of their lives. She felt—and she turned out to be right—that the more open and honest she managed to be, the more honest and open her guests would become.

She went to Ethiopia, where a famine raged, and hosted a documentary produced by WLS-TV. The trip had a lasting effect, for she saw with her own eyes how terrible things were. She saw hordes of children with no food, no hope, no future, nothing but rags and scraps of food on their lucky days.

She had already become a sought-after speaker, especially for teenage groups, and now her message grew even stronger.

Chapter Five

A Remarkable Debut

IN 1985, QUINCY JONES, the musician/composer/arranger/record producer etc., happened to visited Chicago. He caught Oprah's show in his hotel room, and a brilliant idea lodged itself in his ever-active mind.

He had just entered into a co-producing venture, the filming of Alice Walker's powerful novel *The Color Purple*, published and critically acclaimed in 1982.

It tells the story of a black woman, Celie, who grows up in the rural South in the early part of this century, in a world saturated

In 1985, Quincy Jones was searching for an actress to play the role of Sofia in The Color Purple, *the film adaptation of the Alice Walker novel. While in Chicago, he happened to see Oprah's talk show and decided she would be ideal for the part.*

Oprah is seen at right in one of her important scenes in The Color Purple, *the moment when her character, Sofia, insults the mayor's wife, who has been trying to make Sofia work for her*

as a maid. Because of the insult, Sofia is beaten by a group of
white men, and when she tries to demand justice, she is arrested,
tried, and sent to jail herself.

with cruelty. We see her as a child, running through fields of purple flowers with her sister. Then she comes closer. She is pregnant. We find that her father has made her pregnant and will give away the child, as he did with a previous baby.

Alice Walker told the story in a series of letters, some never sent, most of them addressed to God. Writing them is Celie's only way of staying sane in a world where she is ignored or mistreated.

Celie is married to a cruel man whom she calls "Mister" (played by Danny Glover in the film), who brings his longtime mistress, an alcoholic juke-joint singer, Shug, into their home.

An important character in the story is Sofia, a spirited young woman, who is determined to marry Harpo, Mister's son from an earlier marriage. It seems nothing can stop her from achieving any goal she sets up for herself. But her spirit takes a brutal beating, along with her body. That, in combination with being jailed, nearly breaks her.

For the role of Celie, the film's producers and the director (Steven Spielberg) had decided to take a chance on a woman, until then known as a rambunctious comic rather than an actress: Whoopi Goldberg. (She subsequently made her impressive motion picture debut in the fearsomely difficult part, and an acting career was born.)

But no decision had been reached as to who would play Sofia, who serves as the counterpoint to Celie.

Such was the state of affairs when Quincy Jones turned on the television set, flipped from channel to channel in his hotel room in Chicago, and happened to catch Oprah's show.

Seeing the energy and resiliency manifesting itself in the person of Oprah Winfrey, he knew she would be perfect for the role of Sofia.

A week later, Oprah was being interviewed in Chicago and soon was on her way to California to screen-test for the part. She knew Alice Walker's novel well, having read it back in Baltimore and immediately identified with its strong women, perhaps especially with the central character of Celie, a victim of repeated sexual abuse. After "discovering" the novel, Oprah had bought a number of copies and given them to several of her friends.

With the touch of superstition that tends to accompany important mileposts in our lives, and especially in the roller coaster of show business, Oprah saw it as a good omen that the name of her character's husband

Whoopi Goldberg was cast in the principal role of Celie in The Color Purple. *Here she is seen during the filming, receiving direction from Steven Spielberg. This was the beginning of a*

highly successful acting career for Whoopi, who was nominated for an Oscar. Of Oprah, Spielberg has said: "A force of nature. She is absolutely wonderful. Highly intelligent and unafraid."

was Harpo, which just happened to be "Oprah" spelled backwards.

So there she was in Hollywood, and she must have felt like pinching herself. Was she dreaming? Was this reality? Was she actually sitting across from *the* Steven Spielberg, who had made his debut as a feature film director with *The Sugarland Express* in 1974 (at age twenty-six), and whose sixth feature, *E.T.—The Extra-Terrestrial*, had become a major international success two years before Oprah's meeting with him, following on the heels of other tremendous successes (such as *Raiders of the Lost Ark* and *Close Encounters of the Third Kind*)?

Oprah and Steven Spielberg got along from the first. While most people keep speaking about the "cinematic genius" of Spielberg and how his films tend to make enormous amounts of money (*E.T.* grossed $701.1 million, for instance), few take a closer look at his life to discover that he, like Oprah, has taken a far from perfect childhood and adolescence and *remade* himself. His filmmaking (and it began while he was still a child with an eight millimeter Kodak camera) represented an escape from a number of unpleasant realities, at home and at school. He was an indifferent student, a

When Oprah was in her teens, she admired Quincy Jones as a performer, unaware of how greatly he was to influence her life in later years, as friend, mentor, and financial advisor.

social misfit, no good at sports—his classmates called him "the retard."

There might have been a moment of
unspoken recognition between the two when
they met, as there tends to be between people who have overcome the odds against
them.

He might have told her that he had ini-
tially read the book casually and not as a
possible movie project. His producer,
Kathleen Kennedy, had given it to him
because she thought it would enlighten and
educate him.

He read it, and something happened.

"I love this because I'm scared to do it,"
he told the producer.

"I was emotionally transported by the
story and by those people, and I made a
decision the same way I make it on all
movies I decide to direct. It was an impul-
sive decision," he said in 1985, adding: "I
really wanted to make a drama, not so much
to prove to people that I could, because I've
been very satisfied with my career up to this
point, but just to prove to myself that I could
take a story that did not have any upstag-
ing elements like special effects and great
background design and make a movie whose
story was not more powerful than the char-
acters who comprised the story. I wanted to

make a movie about people."

He did find the whole experience enlightening in many ways. "As you know, I was brought up in a very religious home," he said (also in 1985). "It gives you a secure place in your own lifetime, and I think that's what religion does for people. I think there is not a lot of difference between my feelings as a Jew and the feelings I discovered from interacting with the black cast of *Color Purple*. There is a very similar feeling of closeness and family, and it wasn't a foreign experience for me, directing *Color Purple*. I felt very much at home once I got involved in the casting and the actual directing. And I felt at home with these people as part of my family."

He went on to admit that his initial hesitation had to do with his not knowing what part of him could understand a story that was "essentially all black and very rural and very southern and very cultural. I also realized I wanted to make a movie telling a story that wasn't sociological or cultural but was of human nature, and once I really faced that fact, people helped me.

"Alice Walker helped me face this in myself, Quincy Jones helped me, Kathy Kennedy helped me to make this decision. Once I realized I wanted to tell a very, very

One of the most dramatic moments in The Color Purple *occurs when the character of Sofia, played by Oprah Winfrey, is arrested, tried, and sent to jail. In the courtroom, Sofia's hands are*

manacled. In the photo above, an emotional moment in the trial, Sofia rises to her feet to plead with the judge for reason and justice, but her pleas are to no avail.

human story, I absolutely dove into it head first and didn't give a second thought to whether I was going to be erupting a kind of cultural balance."

Having seen several black movies he admired but which had not reached a large general audience, he thought perhaps he could also be somewhat of an inspiration and trailblazer for other black ensemble films. Television had been a forerunner of black ensemble casting, he noted. "And theater, the stage, has been absolutely healthy with black repertoire casting—but movies have not," he pointed out. "I wasn't so pretentious that I said I'm going to be the director that makes this happen..., but if it's a good movie, maybe the film industry will follow and make other black ensemble films, which I think is very important."

Oprah tested for the part of Sofia with Willard Pugh, the actor who was up for the role of Harpo. Spielberg had them read from the script and do a series of improvisations to see how they related to each other. Then he told them simply that they had the parts. Oprah jumped straight up in the air (she has said afterwards), screamed, and hugged Willard; it remains one of the best moments in her life.

And this is what Steven Spielberg had to

say about Oprah Winfrey on December 27, 1985: "A force of nature! She is absolutely wonderful. Highly intelligent and unafraid.

"It is so much more fun finding somebody like Oprah Winfrey, who had a talk show in Chicago, and just deciding that she could play Sofia because of a wonderful test she did for me than to sit with agents for two-and-a-half months and negotiate impossible deals with movie stars. There are movie stars I'd love to work with but I also have this kind of ego about taking somebody who hasn't been seen before and putting them in a movie that brings out their best qualities."

The filming took place in North Carolina and lasted almost three months, during which Oprah's show went on with guest hosts and reruns of her most popular programs. It turned out that Oprah, although lacking experience as a film actress, could hold her own with her experienced co-stars, though she told David Letterman on his show that it was "very intimidating at first."

She went at it with body and soul—the only way she knows how to do things—depicting the headstrong young Sofia. Oprah's character is beaten viciously by the town's white men for having told off the mayor's wife, who had wanted Sofia to come and work as her maid. (Interestingly, it has

In one of the happier scenes of The Color Purple, *Willard Pugh, as Harpo, and Oprah, as Sofia, are married with their child in arms, over the objections of Harpo's ill tempered father, Mister.*

Willard Pugh was the actor Oprah did her screen test with, and his character's name became the name of her production company, when she discovered it was her name spelled backward.

been reported as a tradition in the Winfrey family that none of their women would work as maids for white women.)

One dramatic scene is when a nearly broken Sofia, having served her prison sentence, is sitting at a table, refusing to speak, just rocking back and forth in silence. Then, finally, she does speak—about injustice. One imagines that Oprah Winfrey could identify strongly with that part, as Sofia demonstrates how, no matter what kind of defeats a person experiences, she or he can still become a winner in the game of life. To Oprah, the character might also have represented all those known and unknown black women who are such an important part of our history and who have left her and all women a legacy of strength.

In a story in the *Baltimore Sun*, she is quoted as saying just that: "[Sofia] is a combination to me of Sojourner Truth and Harriet Tubman and Fannie Lou Hamer, and grandmothers and aunts of mine and other black women...."

The film was released in the winter of 1985 and became a huge international success, although it also created considerable controversy.

Some felt that Spielberg had soft-pedaled Walker's raw and angry story, and when

Steven Spielberg looks back, he knows that today he would make it differently in some respects. "There were certain scenes I couldn't bring myself to shoot," he said during an interview in 1993. "Some of the grittier ones..., because I didn't grow up that way.... Or, if I had been a woman, maybe I could have. But being a man, I didn't know how."

Some expressed the opinion that the film was unfair to black men, showing them as abusers of black women. Whatever anybody's view, the film remains one of the utterly few movies of the era to focus on black women.

For Oprah personally, the reviews were enthusiastic. "Shockingly good" and "a revelation," the critics said about her performance.

At Oscar time in 1986, the film received eleven nominations for Academy Awards, including nominations for the two newcomers: Whoopi Goldberg as best actress—and Oprah Winfrey as best supporting actress. (Ultimately, Anjelica Huston won in that category.) Oprah has jokingly said it was a bit of a relief not to win—for a purely practical reason. Between the time her close-fitting evening gown was fitted like a glove on her body and the evening of the awards, pure nervousness had made her add a few extra ounces and the seams were dangerously close to splitting whenever she moved. Walking or running up on stage, lifting the golden Oscar, or even speaking, laughing, or crying could have given everyone a truly intimate look at Ms. Winfrey.

Another example of how far the lonely girl who talked to animals in Mississippi had come occurred the following month when she was one of the guests at the star-studded wedding of Arnold Schwarzenegger and Maria Shriver. She was telling reporters: "When I look at the future, it's so bright it burns my eyes."

Later in 1986, Oprah appeared in the film version of Richard Wright's classic novel, *Native Son*. (Written in 1940, the story takes place in the 1930s.) She played the mother of Bigger Thomas, the frightened young man who unintentionally kills a young white woman. She said once that she based her portrayal partly on her own mother. The critics praised her performance, although the film was not well received generally.

She was not nominated for her role but made it to the Academy Awards show in 1987 anyhow—in a beautifully fitted gown. This time she was there as a presenter, which she found a lot easier on her nerves than being a nominee. "You can concentrate on watching the show, instead of spending three hours making your deals with God, promising to go on a diet, to go to church, to stop biting your nails, and to stay out of shopping malls and everything in between," she said.

Oprah has remained thankful that Quincy Jones "discovered" her. She loves and admires him no end, as an artist and as a person. "He walks in the light," she has said about Mr. Jones, who also scored *The Color Purple*, creating a musical blend of blues, gospel, jazz, and African rhythms.

She and Quincy Jones visited the White House together in the summer of 1994, having been invited to the Clintons' first state dinner. Honored guests were the Japanese emperor Akihito and his empress Michiko. "When I was introduced to her, I didn't know what to say. One of the few times that has happened!" she revealed afterwards. Being tongue-tied was a temporary affliction, however; before long, she and Quincy and Barbra Streisand became the life of the party.

Chapter Six

Success
and Love

OPRAH WINFREY'S Chicago talk show remained hugely successful.

On September 8, 1986, five years to the day after she had written her farewell-to-this-lonely-life note during an attack of depression, her program became nationally syndicated. This was a historic moment: it made her the first black woman with a nationally syndicated talk show.

The syndicating company was (and is) King World Productions, and they declared her program to be "the hottest-selling show" they had ever handled.

In 1986, Oprah was nominated for an Oscar as Best Supporting Actress for The Color Purple, *and soon afterward her show became nationally syndicated. Success was now in her reach.*

It proved to be accurate because, within six months, hers was *the* highest-rated talk show in syndication.

By now, the powers-that-be had begun to discover the enormous power and impact of talk shows, both on radio and on television. Talk shows were rapidly becoming the modern era's electronic confessional.

Numbers such as sixteen million *daily* viewers make one stop and consider some comparisons. For instance, how many people did the great prophets of any religion reach *during their whole lifetimes*?

One reason for the popularity of these programs is that the listener/viewer might feel he or she is an interactive part of the show. This serves to break the feeling of loneliness and isolation that permeates today's society. It is a relief to discover others out there who are just like us, have the same problems and desires; frequently they are worse off than we are, which might help to put our own lives in a better perspective.

People bear witness to the fact that some of Oprah's shows have helped them cope with their own lives. "After all," says a regular watcher, "I see real people with real problems or real victories. I get a lot of useful information and plenty of pure entertainment from it."

One of Oprah's great problems in life had been her weight, until she took up a program of diet and exercise. Here she is seen in New York's Central Park, warming up before jogging.

Oprah figured that those who watched her shared—with her and each other—similar longings, fears, hopes, problems, uncertainties, visions, and dreams. From the first, she demonstrated an uncanny ability to make audiences feel and note what they had in common with her rather than what was different in background or life-style. Her audience might have been largely white, middle-class housewives and mothers; in other words, they were a lot of things she was not. Yet they had much in common with her. They were fellow human beings.

This feeling of unity and identification manifested itself whenever she walked down a street or entered a restaurant: people would greet her like a close, trusted friend.

Once a Chicago policeman saw her trying frantically and unsuccessfully to hail a cab to get to work. He stopped and gave her a ride.

In the middle of a show, she could kick off her high-heeled shoes, sigh, and say, "Ouch, my feet hurt," and there wasn't a woman watching who didn't know exactly what she was feeling. "God is in the details" goes a saying in show business. The details of her show added up to comfort, to an emotional exchange, a sort of group therapy of sharing, resulting in many of her viewers, whoever they were, feeling good when watching her in action.

When Mike Wallace interviewed her for *60 Minutes*, Oprah attempted to explain her success to him: "The reason I communicate with all these people is because I think I'm every woman and I've had every malady and I've been on every diet and I've had men who have done me wrong, honey."

She also said: "I will do well because I am not defined by a show. I think we are defined by the way we treat ourselves and the way we treat other people."

Oprah followed the example of other successful people and formed her own Harpo Productions, Inc. She purchased a large building in downtown Chicago, which houses her up-to-date production studio with tastefully decorated offices, screening room (complete with popcorn machine), and three soundstages. A neon sign proclaims *Harpo Studios*. Oprah herself chose every piece of furniture and also created a fitness center for her staff, as well as a cafeteria with wholesome food. Her own office is a beautiful oasis with flowers, art books, and framed photographs of people she loves, such as Maya Angelou and Quincy Jones.

In the summer of 1986, she also purchased

a high-rise condominium (for $850,000) on the fifty-seventh floor of a gleaming Chicago tower. She has since added another two apartments in order to create her "perfect home." The result is a showplace with a spectacular view of Lake Michigan, and it smartly combines utter elegance with warmth and comfort.

Her home has a sauna, wine cellar, crystal chandeliers, inlaid wood floors, antique furniture, a bedroom fit for a queen with a silk canopy over her French bed, four bathrooms, fresh flowers everywhere, Oriental rugs, and big white sofas. (This last item could have changed since she auctioned off white suede sofas from her home on a recent show, with the proceeds going to charity.)

Her love of earth tones is reflected in the decor, as is her love of art. Prominently displayed is a gift from Bill Cosby—an Elizabeth Catlett sculpture. In the hallway hangs a framed letter from Winnie Mandela: "Oprah! You must keep alive! Your mission is sacramental! A nation loves you."

No wonder she has exclaimed: "It's hard for me to remember drawing water from the well every morning and playing with corn-cob dolls!"

However, as a great number of prosperous and eminent people have discovered,

Until Stedman Graham, Jr., came into Oprah's life in 1986, she had told people who asked about her love life, "Mr. Right's coming, but he's in Africa and he's walking."

you don't get hugs from bank accounts and fame and television ratings. "Mr. Right's coming, but he's in Africa and he's *walking*," she used to tell her audiences. It was her way of noting that, although there was plenty of success in her life, there was a lack of the light and warmth of romantic love.

She was forced to accept the cold fact that she had still not been overly successful in the love department. She has quoted lines from her diary, such as this entry: "Lord, could you do something about this man situation in my life?... Lord, could he be smart? And, if you don't mind, could he be tall?"

Her prayer was answered—in the shape of a handsome ex-basketball player, Stedman Graham, Jr. They began dating in May 1986. Graham is six-foot-five, has a master's degree in education, runs a drug-counseling program for youth, Athletes Against Drugs, and is president of a public relations firm, Graham Williams Group.

She admitted to friends how she felt when she first met him. She thought he was almost too handsome and too good to be true. ("Six-feet-five of terrific," she said when Joan Rivers asked about him.) Some reports claim she turned down the first couple of dates when he asked her out. Old suspicions were awakening in her—partly her early uncertainties about herself, partly every celebrity's query having to do with "Is it me or is it my fame and all it entails?" Steady as they go, Graham did not give up, thereby showing her one side of his personality she found highly positive: determination.

The more she learned about him, the more she liked what she saw, and the happier she was that he had finally worn down her resistance.

Before long, she was able to tell her friends about having found a man who was confident, who had his own identity, who was not after her money, who was fun to be with, who listened to her opinions, who treated her marvelously. "He made me realize a lot of the things that were missing in my life," she told *Ebony*, calling Stedman Graham, Jr., "an overwhelmingly decent man."

Chapter Seven

Another Degree of Success

OPRAH WINFREY'S SHOW had gone into syndication on 180 stations around the nation by September 1986, and it kept presenting an interesting mixture of subject matter.

Her first national show offered advice on how to catch a man. ("Two things have bugged me for years," she told her appreciative audience. "My thighs and my love life!") The next show dealt with fighting families, the third with neo-Nazis, and so on.

Indeed, she was unafraid of controversial

In 1992, during the Los Angeles riots, Oprah took her show on location in hopes of helping ease the racial tension. Here she is seen with noted actor Louis Gossett, Jr., who appeared on one of the shows during that time.

topics and did not worry about straying from the road of "political correctness."

Some will recall a 1987 show where she went to Forsyth County, Georgia, a place known for many racial confrontations since 1912, the year when a white teenage girl was allegedly raped by three black men. No trial; the three were dead immediately upon being accused, and blacks were warned in no uncertain words to get out of the county or else....

This particular show, titled "On Remote in Forsyth County," explored the reigning feelings of hate and mistrust and asked a lot of questions. As it was taped before an all-white audience, there were black protesters picketing outside, charging Oprah with having "turned white." Her reason for having only whites inside was simply that she specifically wanted people of Forsyth county as her audience—and obviously that meant white folks only. Furthermore, she let people speak without censoring them, believing those who were viewing the show would be able to see, hear, and judge accordingly.

Her motivation behind the program was trying to *understand* deep-seated fear and hate in people and to awaken reactions in those who were hearing what was said and seeing those who said it.

This is one reason for her show, in her opinion: information and communication in order to gain understanding (even of what she and any thinking individual cannot endorse in any form—perhaps especially of those manifestations). Only from a basis of understanding what is before us, what is happening around us, can anything be dealt with in a rational, effective way.

She has always been concerned with having shows dealing with difficult situations in which viewers might find themselves, her purpose being to show troubled people that they are not alone. It is important to her not to become some kind of pretentious star of a television show; she wants to remain a guide, a friend, a sister. She does what she feels is right and positive, in one way or another, and it almost always works.

In 1987, her show garnered more attention as it won three Emmy awards—for Outstanding Talk/Service Program, Outstanding Direction, and Outstanding Host.

She was delighted but perhaps even more so about reaching another and more personal goal.

She had left Tennessee State University in 1976 to take the job with WJZ-TV in

Baltimore and consequently had never completed her senior project and therefore had not graduated. Over the years, her father would remind her now and then that she had never received her diploma. So in 1986 she again enrolled at TSU and worked out a project that would satisfy the requirements for graduating.

She received her diploma during the 1987 commencement ceremony—and also addressed the graduating class.

Vernon Winfrey proudly watched as his daughter strode across the stage, was handed her diploma, and announced she was establishing ten annual full scholarships in her father's name.

In her speech, she told the other graduates: "Don't complain about what you don't have. Use what you've got. To do less than your best is a sin. Every single one of us has the power for greatness, because greatness is determined by service—to yourself and others."

In 1988, another honor was given her: she became the youngest recipient of the International Radio and Television Society's Broadcaster of the Year Award.

In November of the same year, Harpo Productions bought *The Oprah Winfrey Show* from the ABC Network.

Oprah has credited her father, Vernon Winfrey, with being an important influence on her life. Even after her success he encouraged her to return to college to complete her degree. Here they are seen together at the NAACP Image Awards ceremony.

She was and is a personification of her message that being born female, black, and poor doesn't mean being denied access to the very pinnacles of success. The necessary ingredients, as she sees them, are working hard and daring to dream.

The hard work and the dreams have continued. A typical Oprah day might look like this: getting up at 6:00 A.M., working out or jogging, shampooing hair, driving to work with wet hair (perhaps in her Jaguar convertible), getting makeup and hair done while discussing the day's program with her producer, greeting the studio audience, taping the program, meeting with staff for business, research, and planning sessions, and getting home at 8:00 P.M.

Variety is the spice of any talk show, and she keeps a constant lookout for new angles, approaches, and ideas.

In 1988 she returned to Kosciusko, Atala County, Mississippi, where the road in front of her childhood home was renamed "Oprah Winfrey Road." As she cut the ribbon during the dedication ceremony, tears were running down her cheeks, and she felt as if she wanted to embrace the whole world. It was a celebration of the road she had traveled from *then* to *now*.

On her show on November 15, 1988, after

a widely publicized diet that lasted for months, she appeared on stage pulling a wagon loaded with sixty-seven pounds of lard to symbolize the weight she had lost.

Chapter Eight

The Acting Bug Bites Again

OPRAH HAD READ and loved the novel *The Women of Brewster Place,* by Gloria Naylor. It tells the stories of seven black women sharing life in the same tenement in a northern city.

She wanted to make a television film based on the story, feeling it was "about maintaining your dignity in a world that tries to strip you of it." She went to the three main networks saying she wanted to co-produce and star in the movie. All three turned her down.

Never taking no for an answer when she

In 1988, Oprah produced the television movie, The Women of Brewster Place, *taking the role of Mattie Michael herself. It was a success, but the spinoff series lasted only ten episodes.*

really wants something, she marched back to ABC, entered the executive offices, and handed out copies of the novel. With the sweetest smile she could manage and in a voice that could melt butter, she told the executives that she knew them to be highly perceptive and had figured the reason they had turned down the project was simply that they had not read the book!

"You could not read it and turn it down. So I'll be calling on you Tuesday to see who has read it. We're going to have a book report, fellas!"

When Tuesday arrived, only one executive had read the novel, but evidently it was enough—the project began to take shape.

By working practically around the clock, she taped four weeks of *The Oprah Winfrey Show* in advance, after which she went to Los Angeles for the filming of *Brewster Place*.

A top-notch cast had been assembled: Cicely Tyson, Olivia Cole, Robin Givens, Moses Gunn, Jackée, Paula Kelly (who also doubled as choreographic dance supervisor), Lonette McKee, Barbara Montgomery, Phyllis Yvonne Stickney, Douglas Turner Ward, Lynn Whitfield, and Paul Winfield.

And of course Oprah, playing Mattie Michael, the maternal sage of the neigh-

The Women of Brewster Place *had an impressive cast. The women were: top, left to right, Olivia Cole, Phyllis Yvonne Stickney, Lonette McKee, Paula Kelly; center, Oprah and Lynn Whitfield; bottom, Jackée, Robin Givens, and Cicely Tyson.*

borhood, who counsels the oft-beleaguered residents of Brewster Place. Again, she gave the part and the work all she had of energy and understanding.

The two-part television movie won the ratings war on two consecutive nights when it aired in 1988.

It was nominated for a prime-time Emmy, and Paula Kelly was nominated for Outstanding Actress in a Supporting Role.

Pleased with the success, the following year, ABC and Harpo agreed to co-produce a weekly series spinning out of *Brewster Place*. Oprah was still playing Mattie, but the series was now set in 1967 so she didn't need the aging makeup, and Mattie had bought a restaurant with her friend Etta Mae.

"It's going to be real—we won't fake life," said an enthusiastic Oprah, who didn't mind her long workdays resulting from doing the series and her talk show.

The series did not do well, however. A majority of the critics didn't like it. Black women in the real world rather than what they *thought* was the "black world"—could that be the reason?

Despite the critics' disliking the series, they acknowledged the quality of the show, and some said it was "too mature for a half-

Paula Kelly was nominated for an Emmy as Outstanding Actress in a Supporting Role for her performance in The Women of Brewster Place. *In addition to her role, she served as choreographer for the film.*

hour program." Might it have found its audience and done better on PBS than on a network?

The show was dropped after just ten episodes. Oprah's company lost around ten million dollars, but that's part of the risk of show business. Personally, Oprah did not consider the series a failure: "I don't believe in failure. It is not failure if you enjoyed the process."

Next her Harpo Productions and Quincy Jones bought the rights to Zora Neale Hurston's novel, *Their Eyes Were Watching God*, a coming-of-age novel from an important writer, the most dominant female figure in the Harlem Renaissance era.

Harpo Productions also bought the rights to Toni Morrison's *Beloved*, about a woman's escape and recovery from slavery, as well as Mark Mathabane's memoir of his childhood in South Africa, *Kaffir Boy*.

The rapidly growing company became part owner of three network-affiliated television stations. Oprah bought an interest in a Chicago restaurant, the Eccentric. When she was asked why, she said her reasons were twofold: she wanted a place where she could get mashed potatoes with radishes, and she needed a place where she could go dancing.

Oprah's Harpo Productions and Quincy Jones bought the film rights to Their Eyes Were Watching God, *the classic novel by the highly acclaimed Zora Neale Hurston, seen above.*

She made another important purchase: a 162-acre farm in Indiana. "I've never loved a place the way I love my farm," she told a reporter. It became her escape, her safety vent—a place to experience peace and quiet, take long walks, get in touch, as it were, with her rural childhood, recharge her batteries, and read a lot. The habit instilled in her as a child remains a constant joy in adulthood; she is an avid, eclectic reader.

We might wonder what it is like to work for the dynamo called Oprah. What kind of employer is she?

In one word—demanding. She is a perfectionist, and she expects others to strive for perfection. She works hard, and she requires her staff to work hard. She only likes to work with individuals who have a strong desire to improve themselves.

She is also generous and regards her staff as part of her family. Bonuses are frequent when work is well done.

She will invent fun ways to show her appreciation. Once she took three producers and one publicist, all women, to New York for a shopping spree. She made a game out of it, giving them, for instance, one hour to spend a certain amount of money in a certain department. Another time she thought up a time-regulated game for them to get their choice of shoes or boots.

The five women were driven around New York in a limousine, laughing a lot, sipping champagne, talking, inspiring each other.

There have been disgruntled employees, lawsuits, and turmoil in general inside her company, some of it caused by the hard hand used by one producer in interacting with co-workers. For a long time, Oprah didn't want to deal directly with the problem, partly because she felt she owed much of her success to this particular producer. Finally she accepted fully her responsibility as head of the company ("and as an adult!") and confronted the situation head-on. The producer left, and insiders reported that a kinder, gentler atmosphere reigned in the halls of production. This was an atmosphere more in step with her personal philosophy and the tone of her shows.

She has frequently said that her mission in life is to help others to reach their goals as she has reached some of hers and keeps striving toward ever new ones.

In one 1995 program, designed to show members of her audience from coast to coast how wishes could come true, she made it possible for one of her staff to realize a dream. The young woman, a publicist, had always wanted to be a singer. Well, Oprah spoke with her friend Patti LaBelle. That warm-hearted diva coached the young woman and gave her the chance to perform in her club, a performance Oprah televised on her show.

She does inspire loyalty. "I'd take a bullet for her," said one of her producers (Mary Kay Clinton) at one time.

Her well-documented generosity includes her biological family. She has long since made peace with her mother, has bought her a luxurious condo, and has largely supported her financially. She has done a lot for her half-sister Patricia and especially Pat's daughters, Oprah's nieces. When her brother was alive, she was helping him out with money as well.

It might be surprising to some that Oprah was able to reconnect with her sister, especially after the aforementioned disclosures Pat had made to the tabloids. For two years after that happened, Oprah refused even to speak to her. Finally, she realized that she couldn't live with bitterness (and she couldn't speak from her heart to her audiences about the healing property of forgiveness). She called a family meeting with her mother, her sister, her sister's daughters, and a cousin of whom she is very fond. During a weekend, they did a lot of talking,

When Oprah wanted to give one of her staff members an opportunity to become a singer, her good friend Patti LaBelle (above) coached the young woman and allowed her to perform at her club, with Oprah televising the performance.

relived a lot of pain, and reached a plateau where they could relate, "if not necessarily as sisters, if not necessarily as mother and daughter, just as woman to woman."

Oprah's father remains her close support in a mutual relationship of trust. He tends to refuse money from her. The only thing he supposedly has asked of her was for tickets to the Mike Tyson–Michael Spinks heavyweight championship fight! She has, however, bought him a beautiful house in Nashville and furnished it splendidly.

The man in Oprah's life, Stedman Graham, has another quality in common with Vernon Winfrey in that he refuses to let Oprah buy him expensive gifts. He, on the other hand, has given her handsome presents, such as a classic car on one birthday.

Charities receive hefty contributions from Oprah. She has established a foundation, Oprah Winfrey Charitable Giving, to manage the steady, heavy flow of requests. "What is the fun of having money if you can't use it to make people happy," is her philosophy, and she lives up to it.

She is helping to feed people in South Africa (a project inspired by Stedman Graham after his visit there) and in the United States through several charities set up for that purpose.

She has a little sisters program, Kidadah (it means "little sister" in Swahili), in Chicago's Cabrini-Green housing projects and has provided the girls living there with library cards in order to encourage them to discover the magical world of books; she visits, she counsels, she takes them to movies and dinners whenever her time allows.

When she visited a skid-row church in San Francisco one Easter, she created a miracle of her own by writing out a check for several thousand dollars. But she did more than that—she went around and talked to crack addicts and alcoholics, shaking their hands, hugging mothers with babies, acknowledging their worth as human beings. She understands that a moment of recognition is vital. Many homeless people begging for change in the street will tell you that it isn't refusal to give money that hurts most, it's when people won't even look at them, thereby rendering them invisible.

She has helped raise money for the Los Angeles Rape Treatment Center and the Urban Women's Shelter in Harlem, as well as a shelter for battered women in Inver Grove Heights, Minnesota; and she has contributed generously to Chicago's Academy for the Performing Arts and Chicago's

Corporate Community School.

When August Wilson's play, *The Piano Lesson* (which was presented in a network movie version on television in 1995), opened on Broadway, she bought all the tickets to one performance and donated them to a Boston organization, A Better Chance, that arranges for needy minority students to attend leading private schools.

Although she prefers little or no publicity around her charity work, quite a few people (especially those on the receiving end) are aware of some of it, simply because she does so much. For instance, in October 1988, her big heart was acknowledged when she was presented with the National Conference of Christians and Jews' Humanitarian Award.

At the time she was deeply involved with giving every kind of support, including financial, to a colleague whom she loved like a brother and who was dying of AIDS. He had been with her for a long time, cheerful and full of ideas, booking guests and assisting in the control room. She realized that all the money in the world didn't make it possible for her to save the life of one of her most cherished friends.

When The Piano Lesson, *a play by August Wilson, starring Charles Dutton and Elfre Woodard, opened on Broadway, Oprah bought all the tickets for one performance, giving them to a charity providing educational opportunities for needy students.*

Chapter Nine

Speaking Up, Speaking Out

"**I**F YOU ARE STRUGGLING and it just doesn't seem to be coming together, you can't look outside yourself for why it isn't working. You have to stop right where you are and look right inside yourself."

Words to that effect are pronounced with sincere emphasis by Oprah Winfrey as she travels around the country speaking publicly to youth organizations or women's groups, telling them that the real enemy is carried within them.

Her introduction to a speech often goes something like this: "I was born in

---

In 1993, when President Bill Clinton was inaugurated, Oprah was invited to participate in the Inaugural Gala. Clinton signed a bill sponsored by Senator Joseph Biden, and campaigned for by Oprah, which required registration of known child abusers.

Kosciusko, Mississippi, around the corner from the Nile and down the street from Kenya. The drums of Africa still beat in my heart."

She is ever "celebrating the journey" of her people—and is also concerned with issues "without color," such as abuse of women and children.

She tries in every way to bring out her strong belief that a human being has the power to renounce and to accept, that a man or a woman can make of himself/herself a pawn or a godlike creature, that we hold our own fate in our hands and thereby ultimately the fate of the world.

She will make personal appearances to speak in support of battered women and rape victims whenever possible, those who have been made into dehumanized commodities and who have to be taught to recapture their innate power over their lives. To deny or simply to wish for things to be different is not enough; the only thing powerful enough to liberate us is a new knowledge about who and what we truly are.

A strong example of the potency of her commitment is what she considers her most important public performance: her testimony before the United States Senate

Judiciary Committee regarding the legislation proposed by her to create a national registry of convicted sex offenders. It would mean that an FBI-administered database would be available to schools and other child-care institutions for the purpose of screening job applicants or employees—with their consent—to eliminate having anyone with a child-abuse history around children.

The bill was prompted by her awareness of the obvious, also verified by experts, namely that pedophiles tend to seek employment where they will be in contact with children. "We must do everything we can to detect those that would hurt children before another tragedy takes place," she told the senators, eloquently citing statistics of more than 2.5 million reports of suspected child abuse and neglect per year.

The recent tragedy she kept referring to in her speech, and which had provided the spark bringing her idea to fruition, was the report of a four-year-old Chicago girl being found molested, strangled, and thrown into Lake Michigan. Her name was Angela Mena. A thirty-one-year-old man, Michael Howarth, who had been convicted *twice* for abduction and rape of children and who had just moved into the apartment next to the girl's mother, confessed to the murder.

Oprah, who didn't know Angela or her family, cried bitterly and said to herself, "I have to do something."

First she devoted a show to the tragedy of child abuse and continued by appearing before the Senate. "I will lobby and work on this issue with the same energy I devote to my television career," she vowed.

She spoke before the Chicago Bar Association. "We seem to have declared war against our children.... I know what I am talking about," she said and went into her own childhood story and her feelings of guilt. "Children cannot stand alone; none of us do." She recounted the story of the little four-year-old girl. "Will you take a stand for the children?" she asked the lawyers in a passionate plea.

President Clinton signed the Oprah-inspired bill, sponsored by Senator Joseph Biden (a Democrat from Delaware) into law in December 1993.

She knows there is more to be done about this and other problems in our society.

One matter about which she is deeply concerned is signs of self-hatred she has noted among her fellow African Americans. She has made comments that have led to some severe—and public—criticism from other blacks. Her concern is based on her knowledge and experience in a personal way, which have taught her that negativity about oneself tends to attract the negative from the world around.

She shares Jesse Jackson's conviction that, while people who are victimized "may not be responsible for being down, they must be responsible for getting up." With him she also shares a deeply rooted belief and trust in the spiritual strength of African Americans, many of whom have proven to have "spirits bigger than their circumstances."

This has been confirmed time and time again; Malcolm X is one shining example. His portrayer on screen, Denzel Washington, said playing Malcolm made him wiser: "Malcolm made a lot of mistakes but he was constantly evolving, constantly growing, constantly getting better. I think that's the essence of the human condition."

To further quote Mr. Washington's Malcolm-inspired wisdom: "Being angry is an easy choice. Knowing yourself takes a little more effort...," and "Don't worry about who hates you or not—get busy with yourself."

In the same spirit, Oprah in her speeches will recommend that her listeners seek the truth within themselves. She also seasons her talks with various other tips for growth: "Surround yourself with people who are as smart or smarter than you!"

Remembering that the best way to avoid criticism is to say nothing, do nothing *be nothing*, it's hardly any wonder she has been attacked from different directions many times. If she didn't take chances, if her show did not create controversy, she and it would be lame, tame, and boring. As it is, people react to her, often strongly, mostly positively, but she is too public a figure not to get her share of half-truths, vicious lies, rumors, and a finger pointed at her for anything that's open to interpretations.

How does she deal with criticism?

Better and better, say those who know her. Like all of us, she has been wounded by some criticism, especially when it has come from the black community, but she has learned from other people in the limelight, people she respects, that the other side of admiration is frequently resentment. She is aware she might make mistakes from time to time but knows they are "honest mistakes." In other words, she is certain of her own motivations for what she does, even if the outcome can occasionally be unexpected. She knows that true success is a journey of learning.

Oprah considered the film Malcolm X *to be an important project, and she has admired the work of actor Denzel Washington, seen here made up for the role of Malcolm in the film.*

Her personal life has not been without its trials and tragedies, most of which have become fodder for the tabloids.

In 1989, right before Christmas, her half-brother, Jeffrey Lee, died of AIDS—at the age of twenty-nine. (She paid his medical expenses through their mother.)

And it was in 1990 that her half-sister went to the tabloids with the news that Oprah had been an unwed teen-age mother whose premature baby had not survived. This was extremely painful, not so much for the revelation itself—she could live with that—but for the sense of betrayal she felt. The fact that a member of her own family had gone out of her way to hurt her, deliberately, was painful.

In an interview in the magazine *Essence* in 1991, she said it also made her realize the burden of guilt she had been carrying around since childhood, and that, in the end, the whole matter had been a test of her faith. "It's easy to have faith when everything is wonderful. Real faith is knowing that, no matter what, you're going to be all right."

She practices what she frequently expresses on her show and in her speeches: "If you live in the past and allow the past to define who you are, then you never grow."

An important part of Oprah Winfrey is her deeply rooted spirituality. She began reading the Bible as a toddler, sitting next to her maternal grandmother; she still reads the Bible. She feels guided and has said that, when things go wrong in her life, it is because she has chosen to ignore her inner knowledge of what is good and not good for her.

Chapter Ten

Still with Her Feet on the Ground

IN 1990, AN ESTIMATED sixteen million American viewers watched *The Oprah Winfrey Show* every day.

The show had also been sold internationally. It aired once a week in Japan and was seen in England, Canada, Holland, New Zealand, Thailand, Bermuda, even in Poland, where it was shown on Sunday nights with Polish voice-overs.

In April of 1989, the *National Enquirer* conducted a reader poll about the best talk show host, "the one who keeps you riveted to the tube." Oprah won overwhelmingly,

---

Under the admiring gaze of the crowds, Oprah arrives with Stedman Graham at New York's Madison Square Garden for the annual Essence Awards, one of many honors given to her during the late 1980s and the 1990s.

pulling 44.4 percent of the vote, or almost double the eighteen percent of number two, Geraldo Rivera. Sally Jesse Raphael was in third place, and Phil Donahue placed fourth.

The same year, *Ms.* magazine chose Oprah as their Woman of the Year "for showing women that we can climb as high as we want to go and inspiring us to take control of our resources and make them work for us and for a better world." Maya Angelou wrote a special tribute: "... success has not robbed her of wonder, nor have possessions made her a slave to property."

Morehouse College in Atlanta, Georgia, bestowed an honorary doctorate of humane letters on her—and in her acceptance speech, she announced she was establishing a scholarship fund by donating a million dollars.

Oprah Winfrey had become one of the wealthiest and most powerful women in America.

She and Stedman Graham received a White House invitation to a state dinner for the prime minister of Australia.

In June 1990, ABC aired an Oprah Winfrey special, *In the Name of Self-Esteem*. She keeps talking about self-esteem because she sees the lack of it as the root of nearly all problems in people's lives. The show fea-

In 1992, Oprah announced her engagement to marry Stedman Graham, Jr., but she continually postponed setting the date. Still their romance continued, and they attended many social functions together, including a dinner at the White House.

tured her talking to a variety of people about the subject: Maya Angelou, Drew Barrymore, a teacher from an inner-city school, a woman managing a treatment center for drug addicts.

She also tied in with ABC's after-school specials for issue-oriented programs about matters of concern to young people, whether it is self-esteem, drugs, sex, makeup, dress, or whatever.

In the fall, the ABC network aired *America's All-Star Tribute to Oprah Winfrey* on September 18. Oprah received America's Hope Award presented by Bob Hope, an award to acknowledge generosity and humanity. Bob Hope had been the first to receive it in 1988, Elizabeth Taylor was the second recipient in 1989. Whoopi Goldberg and First Lady Barbara Bush took part in the tribute to Oprah.

The following month, Oprah and Bill Cosby hosted the Essence Awards in New York, where special tributes were paid to Winnie Mandela and Sarah Vaughan. Oprah was also among the several celebrities in the October 1990 documentary *Listen Up: The Lives of Quincy Jones*. And in December of the same year she was a guest on James Earl Jones' TV series *Gabriel's Fire*.

In 1990, in Palm Springs, California, Oprah was honored with America's Hope Award presented by Bob Hope and filmed for ABC as America's All-Star Tribute to Oprah Winfrey.

In 1991, her show won a trio of Emmys again—for Outstanding Host, Outstanding Program, and Outstanding Director. When producer Debra Di Maio accepted the Outstanding Program award, she thanked Oprah for her "once-in-a-lifetime" spirit, while Oprah thanked the guest featured on the submitted program, a sexually abused woman with a multiple personality disorder. Oprah took pride in this particular program because she felt it had given other victims of sexual abuse a chance "to release some of their personal shame."

In 1992, *Forbes* magazine (a financial periodical) reported that Bill Cosby and Oprah Winfrey were the two top money-making show-business celebrities in the world. This is interesting because the story has been told of Bill Cosby giving Oprah a simple, effective piece of financial advice early on: "Sign your own checks." By these words he was saying: keep control, know where your money is. The examples of celebrities who have lost millions because they have allowed others (accountants, business managers, even members of their own families) to control their checkbooks are legion. Not Oprah. She keeps control. She invests (such as in the Chicago restaurant), she helps, and she has fun with the riches

In 1992, Forbes *magazine reported that Oprah Winfrey and Bill Cosby (above) were the two top money-making show-business celebrities in the world. Early in her career, Cosby gave Oprah advice about money management.*

she has received from being the best she can be.

A lucky woman? Yes, but it has not been just luck. There is a lot of truth behind her statements at times referring to her television program as her "ministry." She has strong beliefs. "Things don't happen at random in our universe," she says.

She works hard, always asking for more from herself. There is an honesty in her that goes to the very core of her being.

With advice from smart men such as Bill Cosby and Sidney Poitier (who once told her she was "carrying the people's dream"), advice she has taken to heart, Oprah is much more involved in her business affairs than many entertainers. Her multi-million-dollar earnings have resulted from gently but firmly practicing the art of leverage insofar as actually owning her own show and owning her own studio. She is only the third woman—and the first black woman—ever to own a production studio. (The first was Mary Pickford, the second Lucille Ball.) Seeing her run the business is "actually inspiring," said a woman on her staff a couple of years ago. "She makes me feel I could do that, too. She has also taught me the responsibility of economic power." To Oprah, "economic power" means that, unless you do

In December of 1990, Oprah made a guest appearance in the television series Gabriel's Fire, *which starred James Earl Jones (above), one of the all-time great actors of stage and screen.*

great things with money, it loses its power.

She firmly believes everyone has the *potential* for greatness in his or her life, and she does not equate greatness with fame. Fame is a by-product and not necessarily a blessing. The constant scrutiny wears one down and often interferes too greatly with the living of life. Nor does she believe that making money is enough as a goal.

In 1992, she made her debut as a theatrical Broadway producer when she, with five others, brought Dr. Endesha Ida Mae Holland's play *From the Mississippi Delta* to the stage. In it, the playwright chronicles a woman's journey from the streets to a PhD.

In May of that year, Oprah and Denzel Washington co-hosted the fifth annual Essence Awards, and the same month she did an ABC special *Oprah: Behind the Scenes,* in which she interviewed Meryl Streep, Dustin Hoffman, and Goldie Hawn. She made another such special in November, in which her interviewees were Richard Gere, Vanessa Williams, and Jodie Foster.

When director Spike Lee's film *Malcolm X* ran out of money while still in production, she joined Bill Cosby, Magic Johnson, and others in helping out. How much did she give? She wouldn't tell. "I simply did what I hope someone would do for me in that sit-

The great basketball star Magic Johnson joined with Oprah and Bill Cosby to provide funds for completing the film Malcolm X. *He has also sought to use his wealth to establish businesses in the black community in Los Angeles.*

uation—and the film is important," she told a reporter.

She was behind an award-winning documentary, *Scared Silent: Exposing and Ending Child Abuse*, in which both perpetrators and victims spoke. She introduced the program by telling her own story. The film aired on the three networks simultaneously, which in itself made television history. It was broadcast again in syndication in December 1994 and resulted in a response similar to the one after the original broadcast, which led to over 150,000 calls to the child-abuse hot line. Oprah and others involved received thousands of letters. "We know from that mail that incidents of abuse were averted, lives were saved," notes producer Arnold Shapiro.

People keep asking and speculating about when she is going to marry Stedman Graham. They announced their engagement back in 1992 but set no date. Oprah just smiles. "We are in no hurry. We're getting married when we're getting married."

For important decisions in her life, she has learned to listen to her own instincts as to the right time. Her days of living and doing things to please others, of being pressured to do what she doesn't truly think is the right thing, are definitely over.

When Spike Lee (above), the writer, producer, and director of many successful independent films, ran into financial difficulties while making Malcolm X, *Oprah joined Magic Johnson, Bill Cosby, and others to provide funds for completing it.*

She keeps appreciating the fact that her man enjoys being with her, giving her special days when it's just the two of them romping around on her farm with horses, sheep, and dogs, walking and talking, not for "show," not in front of photographers or audiences or at gala events, just being together.

However, there are plenty of gala events in her life. Not only did Oprah attend President Bill Clinton's inauguration in 1993; she participated by reading a passage from Thomas Jefferson. Her beloved Maya Angelou read her specially written poem, Diana Ross sang "God Bless America," Aretha Franklin sang, and these talented women moved easily among politicians, power brokers, and other celebrities, including Bill Cosby, James Earl Jones, and Jack Nicholson.

In 1993, her show won the Emmy award for Best Talk Show.

When Michael Jackson decided to give his first live, televised interview, he selected Oprah as the one person he could trust. He did not even want to approve her questions ahead of time.

Oprah Live with Michael Jackson: 90 Minutes with the King of Pop, broadcast from Jackson's ranch, "Neverland," in

In November of 1992, Oprah hosted an ABC special in which she interviewed three guests, a format similar to that used by Barbara Walters, whom Oprah admired. The three were Richard Gere, Jodie Foster, and Vanessa Williams, seen above.

California, aired on February 10, 1993, to an estimated audience of ninety million. It included a surprise visit from Elizabeth Taylor (she and Oprah have formed a mutual admiration society, each calling the other a "brave woman, a humanitarian"). Ms. Taylor had encouraged Michael to open up and do the interview with Oprah.

When Olympic gold medalist Greg Louganis decided in 1995 to speak about the incredible burden of living secretly with AIDS, he chose to tell his story to Oprah.

In April 1993, she threw a lavish sixty-fifth birthday bash for Maya Angelou in North Carolina. Of course, Stedman Graham was there, and so were Cicely Tyson, Quincy Jones, and a host of other friends of the fabulous Ms. Angelou. Oprah had commissioned a special African tapestry with Maya Angelou's portrait woven into the middle as her gift.

After an avalanche of writings about her, she had decided to take pen in hand and tell on paper what she had lived and learned. In June 1993, she attended the American Booksellers Association convention in Miami, Florida, to promote the publication of her autobiography, calling the writing equivalent to ten years of therapy. (She worked with a professional writer, Joan

Michael Jackson granted Oprah his first television interview in 1993, and Oprah devoted a full ninety minutes to the show, Oprah Live with Michael Jackson, *broadcast from Jackson's Neverland Ranch.*

Barthel.) Her publisher, Knopf, had already received advance orders for at least 750,000 copies.

Just weeks later, she suddenly announced her decision not to let the book be published, saying there were too many important discoveries to be made, there was too much learning yet to be accomplished. It took strength to make this decision (the book sales were expected to reach at least twenty million dollars), and she had spent more than a year working on the manuscript.

Perhaps the writing of the book had already accomplished something important, serving as an exercise in confronting her personal demons, the extra baggage she had been carrying around from childhood, the insecurities, the nagging self-doubts, the inability to truly value herself. By reliving her life and thereby really looking at herself without the adornments of fame, success, and riches, there may have been a sense of relief.

She may have perceived the book as unnecessary. For anyone who wants to know more about Oprah, her own show gives a myriad of clues to the real person beyond the public persona.

At the Emmy Awards in May 1994, *The Oprah Winfrey Show* took home trophies for

Ever since being nominated for an Oscar for The Color Purple, *Oprah has participated in the Academy Awards ceremonies. Here she is seen in a publicity shot hugging one of the large set pieces of the coveted award.*

talk show and talk show host.

It's evident she keeps learning from everything. As talk shows in the 1990s have multiplied, most have tried to outdo others with more bizarre and titillating programs.

What about Oprah? What did she do?

While critics labeled most talk shows as "trash TV," "low-fiber fluff," and "talk rot," she did not try to outdo her competition at being more sensational and outrageous. She made an elegant U-turn toward joy!

"I want to empower people," she declared and took off in an inspirational direction without turning her programs into sermons. She is saved from sugary morality by her ever-present sense of humor, which comes out at refreshingly odd times. For example, as a presenter at the 1995 Academy Awards, she struck a model's pose for the cameras in her hard-to-handle chocolate-colored Gianfranco Ferre gown with its poufy net and rustling skirt, then changed into a simpler dress for the rest of the ceremony.

She began to center her show on heartwarming, funny, thought-provoking themes, focusing more on solutions than on problems. "Time to move on from whining and complaining and blaming," she told a reporter. "Enough of focusing on dysfunctioning people. The question is: what are

A svelte and glamourous Oprah Winfrey is seen arriving at the Academy Awards ceremonies, one of the years when she was a presenter. Stedman Graham is seen directly behind her.

you willing to *do* about it?"

She is aware of the risktaking inherent in this road. Some would rather see and hear about the horrible and weird than take a look at themselves and learn steps they can take to change themselves and society. The ratings decide the future of shows, so far as the networks are concerned. Should a few innocent people get hurt in the bargain, it is not considered a strong factor. But it is in the heart and mind of Oprah Winfrey.

"We will last and outlast..., because of our intentions," says she calmly. "I know I'm meant to use my television show as a way of voicing my vision of what the world should be."

Watching her show and her interactions with people, an anecdote comes to mind. "Do we live in the same objective world?" a disciple asked a guru. "Yes, but you see yourself in the world. I see the world in myself." Well, that's Oprah—she sees all others in herself, so of course the lines of communication are open!

She will at times quote the Reverend Jesse Jackson: "Excellence is the best deterrent to racism." And excellence is what she strives for, frequently offers, and wishes to inspire in others.

As a result of her increased confidence in

who she is and what she does, even her yo-yo-relationship to her weight is getting stabilized. Having lost a lot and gained back a lot, she now plays tennis. She also runs. Her first public run was the thirteen-mile mini-marathon in San Diego, for which she registered as "Bobbi Jo Jenkins." After successfully completing it, she entered and finished a marathon race of twenty-six miles, the nineteenth annual Marine Corps marathon, in just under four and a half hours. She is immensely proud of that! "It's the hardest I've ever worked for anything. And the last mile was the hardest." Since she started running in March 1993, her body has become toned and it seems so has her mind, as if the daily challenge of five to fifteen miles of moving has sharpened her mental powers and given her a clearer purpose.

"Running is a metaphor for life. You get out of it exactly what you put into it," she comments.

With a new sense of discipline, and encouraged by her steady, Stedman, she keeps on running and jogging and working out. (Forty-five minutes on the StairMaster and 350 sit-ups are not unusual daily efforts.) She has also been eating a more balanced diet since she discovered the

During the 1992 Los Angeles riots, Oprah filmed a series of shows to help restore calm. In one show, set against a backdrop of a Los Angeles street, she invited Rev. Cecil Murray, pastor

of the First A.M.E. Church of Los Angeles, to discuss problems in the city. Rev. Murray, a leader in the community for many years, had a strong influence, particularly among young people.

woman who is her cook, Rosie Daley. Daley's book, *In the Kitchen with Rosie,* went straight to the top of the best-seller lists because of her involvement with Oprah and the visible results of her cuisine.

Oprah has discovered how much she loves skiing—"It's the next best thing to having wings"—and consequently has bought a house in Telluride, Colorado, a place nestled among tall mountains resembling an Alpine village.

Oprah was making fun of herself and her weight swings in June of 1994 when she invited two thousand of her fans to the Hyatt Regency Chicago for a light breakfast and a benefit sale of dresses and other items from her wardrobe in varying sizes. She began by conducting a silent auction of fifteen special outfits, including the navy blue suit she wore to interview Michael Jackson and the purple sequined dress she wore to the 1985 premiere of *The Color Purple.* More than $150,000 was raised for Chicago's Hull House, a community outreach organization, and Families First, a Sacramento group providing food, shelter, and education for abused children.

In 1995, realizing that her former weight problem was something many could identify with, she started a Spring Training program and even went into cyberspace to stimulate others to do something about their physical health.

She has not given up her acting/producing career. In November 1993, Harpo produced a television movie, *There Are No Children Here*, which was set in a Chicago housing project. The movie, based on Alex Kotlowitz's best-seller, starred Oprah and Maya Angelou and was directed by an African-American woman, Anita W. Addison. It is the true story of two brothers, Lafayette, eleven, and Pharoah, nine, (played by Mark Lane and Norman Golden II, respectively), growing up in world of drugs, shootings, and gangs. Oprah played LaJoe Rivers, their mother, a woman abandoned by her husband, living in a dingy, leaky, cramped apartment, where stray bullets sometimes flew through the window, fiercely determined to save her sons from the street.

"A fine performance, all understanding and restraint," said one review about Oprah's acting. "A modulated and strong performance," said another critic.

Originally she had wanted Diana Ross for the part but, when it didn't work out, she jumped in herself at the last minute—and donated her salary to a scholarship fund for the very housing project where the story had taken place.

An idea was born during the filming. Moved by what she had witnessed, she pledged six million dollars to help one hundred Chicago families break the cycle of poverty. She hoped to be able to take the program nationwide by enlisting corporate sponsors. "No one does it alone," she says. In September 1994 she launched Families for a Better Life, with the aim to give poor urban families $30,000 a year for up to two years, along with day care, education or job training, health care, and counseling.

"People have to be taught how to break the chain of poverty for themselves," she proclaimed. "We are taught to be a victim—we can be taught *not* to be one." She pointed out that the goal was "to give them the bootstraps so they can pull themselves up and out."

The response to this program was overwhelming. More than twenty thousand calls were made to a social service agency. "You can hear the pain in their voices, but you can also hear the hope," said one assistant.

"Every year I ask God for something," she told *TV Guide* in the beginning of 1995. "In 1994, it was clarity..., I also learned that you have to be careful what you ask for, because when you get it, the form may not be exactly what you had in mind, not quite what you were expecting..., I would say 1994 was a time of profound change for me—emotionally, spiritually, and physically."

So what did she ask for in 1995? "Peace and a little joy. I was going to ask for wisdom. But I thought, No, I'll let another year pass before I ask for that, because I'm not sure I'm ready to see what will have to happen to bring me wisdom...."

At the Daytime Emmy Awards, May 19, 1995, she and her staff had reason to celebrate: *The Oprah Winfrey Show* earned best talk show honors for the seventh time. Oprah grabbed her sixth award as top talk show host—so her idea of staying out of the talk-show gutter and aim to uplift viewers by treating people with respect was working. (Further evidenced in 1996 when her show won yet another Emmy.)

After her appearance before the Senate on behalf of children, Senator Joseph Biden told her: "I look forward to your announcement to run for public office." Congressman Don Edwards said: "She knows the things people fear and the things they love. She's astonishing really, and she's good for the country."

She is called one of the nation's most powerful women, but to her the important thing is that she has gained power over herself. She told an interviewer: "I still want what I've always wanted. I used to write it in my diaries when I was fifteen years old, and I'm still writing and saying it all the time. 'I just want to be the best person I can be.'"

She has indeed taken her own advice to others: "You have to be responsible for claiming your own victories. Your past might have been horrid but you can't let victimization in your past define who you are."

She knows what it is to be poor and she is not ashamed of the fact that she is rich today because she did it on her own, trusting her own talent, intelligence, and tenacity. She sees herself realistically, without exaggerated pride or modesty. "I still have my feet on the ground; I just wear better shoes."

CHRONOLOGY

1954 Born on January 29 in Kosciusko, Mississippi.

1960 Moves from her grandmother's farm to Milwaukee, Wisconsin, to live with her mother, Vernita Lee, and half-sister Patricia.

1968 Goes to live permanently with her father and stepmother, Vernon and Zelma Winfrey, in Nashville, Tennessee.

1970 Wins first place in the Tennessee District of the National Forensic League Tournament.

1971 Wins the Miss Fire Prevention beauty pageant in Nashville; becomes part-time newscaster for the Nashville radio station, WVOL.

1972 Wins the Miss Black Nashville beauty pageant and a four-year scholarship to Tennessee State University; graduates from East High School; wins the Miss Black Tennessee pageant; enters university.

1973 Becomes news co-anchor at a Nashville television station, WTVF-TV.

1976 Is offered and becomes TV feature reporter and news co-anchor for WJZ-TV in Baltimore, Maryland.

1977 Becomes the co-host of WJZ-TV's morning talk show, *People Are Talking*.

1983   Relocates to Chicago to host WLS-TV's talk show, *A.M. Chicago* (top-rated in one month).

1985   Feature acting debut, *The Color Purple*.

1986   Nominated for an Academy Award as Best Supporting Actress for her performance in Steven Spielberg-directed *The Color Purple*; her show, now named *The Oprah Winfrey Show*, is expanded to national syndication; forms Harpo Inc. production company; acts in the film *Native Son*.

1987   Receives her degree from Tennessee State University; *The Oprah Winfrey Show* wins three Daytime Emmy Awards; receives the Broadcaster of the Year Award from the International Radio and Television Society; hosts first TV special, *A Star-Spangled Celebration*.

1988   Harpo Productions produces *The Women of Brewster Place*, a two-part television movie; her talk show wins an Emmy; she is presented with the National Conference of Christians and Jews' Humanitarian Award.

1989   *Ms.* magazine chooses her as Woman of the Year; *The Oprah Winfrey Show* wins double Emmys (Best Talk Show, Best Host).

1990   ABC airs *In the Name of Self-Esteem*; receives America's Hope Award on *America's All-Star Tribute to Oprah Winfrey*.

1991   Testifies before the U.S. Senate Judiciary Committee regarding her proposed legislation to create a national registry of persons convicted of sexual abuse crimes against children; her show wins triple Emmys; debuts as off-Broadway producer with *From the Mississippi Delta*; wins Image award.

1992   Announces her engagement to Stedman Graham; does two ABC specials, *Oprah: Behind the Scenes*; her show garners two Emmys (Best Talk Show, Best Host).

1993   Attends President Clinton's inauguration; interviews Michael Jackson on television; President Clinton signs her proposed bill into law; Harpo produces *There Are No Children Here*, a TV movie, co-starring Oprah and Maya Angelou; takes home an Emmy as Best Talk Show Host.

1994   Two Emmys (for show and host); launches Families for a Better Life (to help break the cycle of poverty).

1995   Her show wins Best Talk Show Emmy for the seventh time, she wins Best Talk Show Host for the sixth time; signs multi-picture deal with Walt Disney Company.

1996   Image Award; Foster Peabody Award; *The Oprah Winfrey Show* wins its eighth Emmy.

BIBLIOGRAPHY

Beaton, Margaret. *Oprah Winfrey: TV Talk Show Host*. (Chicago: Children's Press, 1990.)

Bly, Nellie. *Oprah! Up Close and Down Home*. (New York: Zebra Books, Kensington Publishing Corp., 1993.)

Mair, George. *Oprah Winfrey: The Real Story*. (New York: Birch Lane Books, Carol Publishing Group, 1994.)

Nicholson, Lois P. *Oprah Winfrey: Entertainer*. (New York–Philadelphia: Chelsea House Publishers, 1994.)

Waldron, Robert. *Oprah!* (New York: St. Martin's Press, 1987.)

INDEX

PICTURE CREDITS

ABOUT THE AUTHOR

MARIANNE RUUTH is the author of numerous books, including *Sarah Vaughan*; *Stevie Wonder*; *Eddie* [Murphy]; *The Supremes: Triumph and Tragedy*; *Cruel City: The Dark Side of Hollywood's Rich and Famous*; *Bill Cosby*; *Frederick Douglass*; and *Nat King Cole*. She is a former president of the Hollywood Foreign Press Association and is a contributing writer and researcher for *The Twentieth Century* and *The Chronicle of America*. Currently she lives in Los Angeles and reports for newspapers and magazines in France, Portugal, Scandinavia, and other European countries, with an emphasis on the cinema. She has chaired Women in Film International and is a member of Mensa.